Spell & Blade

Sam LW Cox

Acknowledgments

I would like to thank the following for their help in getting my work ready for publishing:

- ➢ Emily G (proofreader/editor)
- ➢ Grayson M (proofreader/editor)
- ➢ Travis T (proofreader/editor)
- ➢ Salvador A (proofreader)
- ➢ AgentGiallo (proofreader)
- ➢ Daniel Lima (artist)
  daniel.cruz/oliveiira@hotmail.com

Contents

Prologue: Life Before the Incident

"We'll need to confirm your name and relation to the deceased in order to continue."

"Clyde Galkerson.... I'm his only son."

The man flipped through his paperwork and placed a few documents in front of Clyde along with a pen.

"I need you to sign here and put your social security number over here and we'll begin reading the will," said the lawyer as he pulled an envelope from his bag and flipped through the contents of the packet.

"Right, so let's begin... ahem."

The lawyer put his reading glasses on as he was pre-reading the papers. He had a very serious expression on his face and the wrinkles on his forehead reached further to the top of his bald head as he read the documents.

"Alright, here we go. I, Rodger D. Galkerston, hereby leave the following to my only son, Clyde

Galkerston: my house, vehicle, and the contents in my safe held at the bank."

Setting the paper down, the lawyer let out a large sigh.

"Unfortunately, there are a few complications," said the lawyer as he took his glasses off to look at Clyde eye to eye. His face had either worry or pity written all over it but Clyde couldn't tell which.

"What complications," asked Clyde, unsurprised as he predicted as much.

"Well, it seems as though he had quite a few medical bills that have already been sent to various collection agencies as well as some unpaid loans through the bank in question. As a result, the bank has claimed the things in his will as collateral."

"I see, is there anything else you need from me," asked Clyde, beginning to get up and leave.

"Well, not from me; however, from what I can tell, you don't owe anything else to the bank but since you were the co-signer on the medical bills, it seems as though you are now responsible for paying for them. I tried to get them dropped but it's out of my hands," said the lawyer leaning back in his chair as if defeated.

"That's fine. I appreciate your help. I will be sure to make it right with you."

"Well, about that..." He leaned forward holding a business card out to Clyde.

"I'm gonna drop my fees. It is the least I can do to help you out, Kid. If you find yourself in some kind of legal trouble, give me a call. I'll help if I can."

"Much appreciated. I'll be sure to keep that in mind."

Clyde took the card, put it in his pocket, and left the office.

****

A few months later

****

"The days seem to drag by here recently," sighed Clyde as he got ready for work.

Fumbling around his one-room apartment doing the same routine he has done since the week his father's funeral was concluded. Which was as follows: wake up, get ready, drive to his first job, then straight to his second job, then back home to sleep, eating cheap noodles and drinking tap water. On his days off, he would do odd jobs for some of the neighbors who kept asking for help with things. His money would go to pay off the bills that his father couldn't.

This morning was a bit different. Clyde began reminiscing about his childhood— about his father. His dad was ex-military, and his mom left him right after Clyde was born. Although he was a devoted father, he was different. He was what people would call a prepper and he enjoyed passing his hobby to his son. They would take camping trips for weeks at a time with only a knife and a tarp. It seemed cruel but, in all honesty, those camping trips were what Clyde missed the most these past few months. He learned from his father how to fight, forge his own weapons and armor, and survive in not only the wilderness but also the real world. Unfortunately, the only thing Clyde didn't have was a strong social life. His dad got moved around a lot because of the military. Clyde didn't get to connect with many people. About a year ago his father was diagnosed with late-stage cancer, Clyde had found him collapsed and even though they did all they could, it was too late.

"I'm gonna be late. I had best get a move on," said Clyde as he caught himself bringing the past back up in his mind.

He woke up well before the sun had a chance to rise in order to make it to work on time and usually skipped the bulk of the traffic this way; however, this morning just felt off as he climbed into his car to begin his commute.

"Seems like winter is coming quickly this year," he said as he turned on the defrost in his car and began to drive.

On his normal route, there was always a point in town he disliked. If the timing was off, then he would surely get stopped by every stoplight on the route. This was one of those mornings. Red would turn to green, green to yellow, and there he was— stopped looking at the red of a traffic light. He waited patiently for the light to turn green. He then proceeded forward. All of a sudden, he heard a *screeech!!* All he saw next was a bright light and then nothing but blackness as a car had undeniably hit him.

Chapter 1: Waking Up

"What happened," asked Clyde as he regained consciousness.

He opened his eyes, but they were met with the blinding bright sky which took a minute to adjust to.

"I'm outside? That doesn't seem right."

As he regained his vision, he looked at what he was laying on. To his surprise, he was laying on rock and sand. Clyde began to look around his surroundings, there were large rocks and hills with patches of grass here and yonder as well as a few trees. None of the landscape seemed familiar to him. Where was he? All of a sudden, he heard a loud *crunch* coming from the direction his feet were pointed. No sooner than he looked towards it, something big jolted towards him. Out of instinct and luck, he kicked at a joint of the beast's leg. The beast fell to its knees with a large slam. Once the dust settled, Clyde noticed a large sword-shaped object had barely missed his head and penetrated the ground right next to it. In a quick fluid motion before the creature could react, Clyde tucked his knees to his chest and kicked with all his might launching the creature just far enough off of Clyde for him to jump to his feet and finally get a look at his attacker.

This thing seems straight out of a cheesy horror movie, Clyde thought as he examined the creature.

It stood just taller than Clyde, around six and a half feet tall. The upper part of its body resembled a praying mantis with blades instead of hooks on its arm and what seemed to be the lower half of some type of beetle. It was the same beige color of its surroundings which would make it easy to miss if it wanted to hide.

The creature had regained its footing rather quickly and seeing that Clyde was now standing, it seemed to take a fighting stance holding its sword-like arm as if it was planning to thrust it through Clyde.

Noticing its intentions, Clyde carefully patted his waist area hoping he had a weapon of some kind, and to his surprise not only did he have weapons, but the handles had a familiar feel to them. He couldn't confirm his suspicion about them because he didn't want to take his eyes off of the creature and give it an opening to attack. He drew the smaller blade of the two and in his peripheral, he confirmed it was a kukri-style blade which was a good start he thought as he took a stance to counter the creature's next attack. No sooner than he did, the creature crouched down and then sprang out like a gunshot towards Clyde.

Just as it got into range, it thrust its sword-like arm straight toward Clyde's chest and in an instant, Clyde parried the thrust with the kukri and advanced closer using both of their momentums to thrust the blade into the joint of the creature. However, before he could jerk it back out, the creature turned and swung its other bladed arm forcing Clyde to retreat leaving his kukri. He didn't retreat fast enough as the creature's slash dug deep into his armor. Clyde retreated further to give himself distance to think, drawing what seemed to be an arming sword as quickly as he got out of the creature's range so he would be ready for its next attack.

This armor is the armor I made years ago. How do I have it? No matter, I've got to find this thing's weakness and kill it before it kills me, then I'll worry about how I got into this situation." As the thoughts raced through Clyde's mind, he readied himself to kill the creature.

After the creature failed at trying to remove the kukri, it had decided to finish the task at hand as it took a noticeably different stance than it had before, crossing its arms as if it were mimicking a samurai with a sheathed sword.

The way this thing fights is like it's used to fighting humans. I'm just gonna have to see if I can bait it into opening up enough for me to land a killing blow, thought Clyde as he raised his sword hoping to fake the creature into stopping an overhead attack.

Sure enough, the creature did as predicted and fell for the bait with its wounded arm. Clyde drew back and quickly went for a sweeping slash that got blocked by the creature's remaining arm. The creature motioned as if it was gonna strike with the free wounded arm, but it came to a jerking stop as if the pain just hit it. Taking the small opportunity, Clyde stepped to the creature's good side getting free from the sword clench and thrust his sword deep into the joint under the creature's good arm until the blade protruded through its eye. It let out a screech that made Clyde lose his hearing for a moment, then it fell to the ground limp and lifeless as Clyde had hoped.

"Phew. This was definitely not what I expected when I woke up. I guess it's time to assess my situation and figure out what's going on… but first I need to make sure this thing isn't gonna get back up," said Clyde exhausted from the fight.

He then unstuck his kukri and sword and began dismembering the creature hoping to get himself some food and see if its exoskeleton would be useful.

"Well, now that that's done, let's see what we've got here," said Clyde cleaning his blade.

There's plenty of meat. I should wait before trying to eat any though in case it's poisonous. As for the shell, it's tough. I'll pack the meat in the upper section so it's easy to carry. I should tinker with all this when I get out of here. I can only imagine what I can make with it. Unfortunately, the lower half is just too for me to carry right now. I'll try to remember where it is later. Looking closer at the blade arms, it seems I've damaged them too much with my sword so they must be about as strong as mild steel and quite heavy as well.

Clyde then began assessing his surroundings in hopes of figuring out where he's at in order to know which way to go. He also inspected his armor and weapons to find out just what kinda damage was done.

"There's no doubt about it, this mark proves that this armor is the set I made for myself a couple years ago. I ended up selling it soon after. Luckily that thing didn't slice all the way through it. It should be easy to fix. This sword is the best sword I ever made; I didn't have it for very long because someone I was showing it to bought it. This kukri is the one I made to take camping. Whoever left me here definitely went through a lot to do all of this. Hmmm... based on the landscape I must be somewhere in the Midwest... I guess the best thing to do is pick a direction and go till I find a road or town."

Clyde got up and slung the meat and shell over his back and looked to the sky.

"If that's the morning sun, then north should be this way. However, the terrain seems easier to traverse towards the south and I'll try to stay high unless I find a water source to drink from."

Clyde walked all day, only stopping to look for water and make sure he was still going in the right direction. It eventually started to get dark. Clyde decided that since the moon was bright tonight, he'd better keep walking. About two hours after walking in the dark, Clyde smelled something in the wind.

"Is that smoke? Someone must be camping nearby," said Clyde as he immediately went to the highest vantage point he could see in order to find the fire.

After reaching the top, Clyde saw a fire in the valley below him in an open field of sorts. The relief Clyde first had turned to dismay.

"Those people are using bows and swords which means that I must be in a different time altogether... They are also surrounded by the same type of creature that attacked me this morning which means that they must hunt in packs of some sort," said Clyde as he watched one of the creatures emerge from the darkness and prepare to attack.

"I wonder if they have a special way of dealing with these things that I didn't think of..." As soon as Clyde said that to himself, he heard what sounded like a loud cicada noise which must be coming from one of the creatures.

Immediately following it, the rest of them joined in, making the sound echo across the valley sending chills down Clyde's back. Clyde snapped back to reality at the sound of screaming and clashing of metal. As Clyde looked back at the light to see what happened, it was over. The creatures were victorious, tearing the victims' limbs off and putting them on their backs instead of immediately eating them. Clyde watched quietly as they finished and in unison disappeared into the darkness heading away from Clyde's perch.

"I'd best stay awake tonight. I don't wanna end up finding out where they went."

Clyde stayed up all through the night watching as the fire slowly flickered out in the distance and making sure he didn't get ambushed in the night. Eventually the sun finally rose, and he made his way cautiously down to the camp of the unfortunate group of people. Once there, Clyde found some much-needed water skins as well as what seemed to be some moldy loaves of bread which Clyde figured was better than mysterious bug meat. He also had found some letters and maps, but the letters were written in an unrecognizable language, and the maps didn't seem to match the terrain.

"Hmmm. It seems as though they came from the direction I'm going so there must be a town or village somewhere if I follow their tracks. But at the same time, that would make me an easier target to be hunted down by those things."

He debated for a moment but decided it would be better for him to not follow the tracks directly and go atop a ridge that followed the valley they walked through so Clyde could clearly see if anything was following him or not.

He walked till about midday and decided that he should try to sleep for a bit so he could stay on guard for another night. After finding a small hollowed out cave that was just big enough for Clyde and his gear to fit snugly, he blocked the entrance with some brush and slept till the cold of night woke him.

He stayed in the small crevice throughout the night listening to the sounds echoing through the night air. All of a sudden, he heard the distant loud chirping that the creatures did the night before followed by many others. Although they seemed far away, it still made Clyde quite uncomfortable as it went on throughout the night longer than it did before. Clyde was curious as to why but knew better than to go investigate.

As the morning sun lit up the mouth of Clyde's little crevice, he finally wallowed out and continued along the ridge. At midday, he saw more smoke in the distance in the direction he was heading.

"I'm not too keen on getting too close after the last incident I witnessed," said Clyde to himself as he walked toward another vantage point.

Once there, he gazed over in the direction of the smoke and to Clyde's relief, he saw a town. The smoke in question was coming from various chimneys more than likely due to it being lunch time. Clyde saw a path leading into the town, so he made his way down and entered.

Clyde's first impression of the place was quite positive despite it sealing the fact that he's definitely not in Kansas anymore. The buildings were made of stone and wood which meant they used what the land provided. There were two- and three-story buildings so if Clyde's knowledge of the medieval days was correct, this town would be considered prosperous, and he wouldn't have trouble finding food and information.

As he got to where people were busying about the streets and stalls were present, he noticed that he was getting some hard looks by the locals as if they couldn't believe they had an outsider among them which made Clyde uncomfortable. His eyes caught a weapons stall, and he went to see if he could get any information.

"Hello there, stranger. Wish to look at my wears," asked the large old man that had more wrinkles than he had things to sell.

"I'm afraid I don't have any money on hand. Would there be any way you could help answer a few questions for me though," asked Clyde, glad that there wasn't a language barrier.

"Hmmm..." the man looked Clyde over as if he were estimating his value, then he closed his eyes for a moment before answering.

"Did you come from No Man's Land boy," asked the man in a concerned but serious tone.

"If that's what you call the place north of here, then I suppose"

"How did you make it through on your own, past all the Gex. There's not many people able to cross No Man's Land, especially manage it alone." The man leaned forward, seemingly expecting some grand explanation.

"Well, I'm not quite sure what a Gex is but to be honest, I woke up in the place and simply made my way out."

"A Gex, my boy, is what those body parts slung over your back belong to. For you to have them must mean you managed to kill one which is no small feat." The man motioned for Clyde to hand over the parts, which Clyde did. The old man continued.

"If this one was by itself when you fought it, it's quite impressive. Means you beat an exiled Gex. Don't get me wrong, it's impossible to fight a whole pack but if you managed to kill an exile one-on-one, it's pretty impressive."

"What's so impressive about it," asked Clyde as he watched the old man fiddle with the shell.

"An exile is more than likely starving which means that it won't mess around when it's hunting; they are usually more aggressive and harder to kill as well. So, if you're willing to sell these... I'll give you a good deal."

"Let's hear your offer," Clyde said, stiffening his expression to hide his emotions. As he did, he noticed that the old man was far ahead of him in both timing and ability. As soon as business hit the conversation, the old man's expressions were stone cold.

"Hmm... I can afford to offer 5 and 3/4th gold neros," said the old man, expressionless as he pretended to be distracted with the shell. It was nothing but an act as he was paying attention to the deal closely.

Clyde stroked his chin as he quickly assessed his options.

For one, I can take the money and try to figure out how the currency in this world works on my own.... or maybe I can throw him off with a different offer that'll help me get the information I need to survive here, thought Clyde as he watched the old man tinker with the shell until... BAM!! The old man dropped the shell loudly on the table and leaned toward Clyde making strong eye contact.

"Well, what'll it be, boy," said the old man, trying to be impatient.

Clyde knew he couldn't lose his composure and simply stared into the old man's dull blue eyes as he decided on his counteroffer.

"How about this," Clyde said, then adjusted his posture before continuing.

"If you provide me food and a place to sleep as well as access to your forge, I'll let you have it."

The old man was genuinely surprised to the point he couldn't hide it. As the shock hit him, he jolted an answer out.

"Y-you've got a deal, son," said the old man as he extended his hand to confirm the deal. Clyde quickly accepted his hand which was quite rough and calloused, proof that he indeed worked hard at his trade.

"It's a slow day as it is... If you'd like, I'll take you to the forge now."

"Thank you, if it's not an inconvenience that would be great," said Clyde, picking up the remainder of his things

"No trouble at all," said the man as he slammed his shudder on his stand.

He emerged from behind the stand shortly after with what seemed to be the bladed shell of the Gex wrapped in cloth and slung over his shoulder.

They began walking down the busy street dodging the busy towns folk running to and from about their busy days. There were fields visible from town; however, they were still quite far from the village, probably near a water source. Craftsmen were busy fixing wagons and houses. Clyde noticed something odd as he curiously looked at the busy craftsmen. A couple was carrying a stone so large a wagon couldn't hold it. Then down the street that was lined in oil lamps, there was a man lighting them by flinging a spark from his hands up to the light!

"Hey, old man..." said Clyde as they walked closer to the lamplighter.

"What is it?"

"How is he lighting those lamps," Clyde asked, walking behind the slowly paced man.

"Huh.... Oh Ferik? He's using a bit of pyromagic. Have you not seen it before," asked the old man gazing off at the Lamplighter as they walked closer.

"Interesting..." mumbled Clyde as he diligently followed the old man while watching the Lamplighter work.

As they continue to walk through the town, the buildings become progressively more rundown with shifty eyes and vagrants dotting the alleyways and gutters. The streets went from a packed stone path to gravel and mud. Before long, the old man stopped in front of an old two-story townhouse with a well-made chimney attached to one side.

"This is it. Come, I'll show you to the forge," said the old man as he entered the house.

The inside was very homely with various trinkets and things the old man must have made hanging along the walls and on shelves. The old man pointed to the room to the side and directed Clyde to enter.

"Honey, we have a guest tonight so make an extra portion for dinner," yelled the old man after Clyde entered the room he was told to.

"I'll have to go to the market then if I have to cook for company," came a woman's voice which had an irritated tone from the far room.

The room Clyde was directed to was indeed his forge with everything one would need to make what he would need. A small fire flickered from within the forge itself. Tools lined the wall on one side and unfinished weapons and tools lined the other wall. A heap of what seemed to be coal was beside the forge and in front of it was a large anvil with a stool beside it. The old man walked over and eased down on the stool and looked up to Clyde.

"So, tell me, boy, why would you turn down such a good offer for something you could have had enough money to pay for things a few months," said the old man with a concerned look on his face.

"Well, to be honest, I didn't specify any amount of time if you recall. So, I could be here a while," said Clyde as he set down his things with a smirk on his face.

"I see… However, seeing as you were also unfamiliar with fire magic, there's something that's not quite adding up with you," the old man prodded further.

Clyde was caught off guard by the sudden interrogation and simply stayed silent.

"Listen, I'm sure you don't trust me and all, but I am letting you stay under my roof even though you paid for it, you can still humor an old man's curiosity. Who knows, maybe I can help you out somehow."

Clyde pulled over a chair that was in the corner and sat facing the old man. As he shared his story, the old man's expression didn't change. After Clyde finished, the old man leaned back and closed his eyes for a moment before replying.

"Well, that's quite an interesting tale. I can understand why you were hesitant to share. Most people would think you're crazy."

The old man thought for a moment and then gave a nod before continuing again. "I've decided then..."

"Decided what exactly," asked Clyde as he was increasingly confused.

"I've decided to help you learn the ways of this world. I'll answer all the questions I can and help you get on your feet so that you can figure out what path you will take. Since I'm gonna be helping, I suppose we should start with names." The old man smiled widely as he reached out his hand for a proper introduction. Clyde accepted his hand quickly.

"The name's Skaald Everflair, son of Emerhald, the best blacksmith in the town of Cleftrock. You may call me Skaald."

His introduction was very practiced and assertive, and Clyde prepared to copy his introduction.

"I'm Clyde Galkerston, son of Roger. You may call me Clyde."

"That's a strong name boy... I'd work on that title though, if you're gonna do any business."

"I will for sure. I appreciate that you're going to help me. I'll be sure to repay your kindness."

"Don't worry about it. By the way, what are the questions you have for me at the moment?"

"Well, I found a small group of travelers that had been killed by a pack of Gex and found this note; unfortunately, it's written in a language I can't read," Clyde said as he dug out the letter and produced it to Skaald.

"Hmm. This is the common script. It's a bounty to hunt a rogue pack of Gex which obviously was too much for them. This group passed through town a few days ago. It's a shame they didn't make it. Can you not read?"

"Well, I can read; however, the script from my world is very different so I'm gonna have to learn to read all over again."

"Hmm. I can teach Dwarvish better than Common, but my wife should be able to help teach you to read Common. She keeps up with my business ledgers and contracts," said Skaald scratching his head.

"I would very much appreciate it... Are you not human," asked Clyde before he thought it might be rude.

"Oh no, no. I'm taller than most of my Dwarven kin because I'm half dwarf, half forest elf. Are there not many dwarfs from your home," asked Skaald, pointing to his pointy ears under his long matted or burned hair.

"No, there's only humans from my world. I apologize if I was rude..." said Clyde embarrassingly.

"I see. That's quite an interesting tale. I would be careful because some people are quite proud of their race. It's best to just not bring it up unless the other party does."

"Understood. Well, if it's okay, I'll begin tending to my armor and weapons. It'll give me time to come up with more questions."

"Of course. Please use the forge to your heart's content. I've got a few more things to take care of before dinner anyway. If you need me, I'll be back in the market," said Skaald as he got up and dusted off the anvil he was leaning on.

Clyde thanked Skaald again and after he left, he went to the grindstone first and wet it and began sharpening his sword and kukri. He lost himself in thought and time passed faster than he knew when he heard something from the other room.

"Come and eat dinner. It's ready," came the voice of a woman snapping Clyde back to himself. He quickly cleaned up his blades and put them away as he began heading towards the kitchen.

Once he opened the door, he was stopped dead in his tracks with shock and amazement at what he was witnessing.

"Oh, it's nice to finally meet our guest.... Is there something the matter," asked the lady as she looked at herself then back to Clyde.

Clyde couldn't find his tongue as he felt that he was in some sort of trance. When he walked through the door, he glanced over at the woman sitting the table. She was wearing a nice, homely dress with a tattered blue apron which matched her scales. Her eyes were almost a glowing yellow and her smile was filled with sharp teeth and swishing along, just visible from behind the table, was a long tail. The words from Skaald instantly came to Clyde's mind, *"It's best not to bring race up unless they do first."* Clyde quickly racked his brain to come up with something nice to say before she got the wrong idea.

"Yo... your scales are quite stunning," said Clyde, instantly wishing he had just stayed quiet

"Oh, oh thank you, that's quite flattering," she said as her cheeks noticeably turned purple in color.

"Please sit down and eat. I'll go fetch some water from the well. Skaald should be home any moment now," said the lady as she picked up the large wooden pitcher.

"Thank you so much... would you mind telling me your name? Skaald forgot to mention it... I'm Clyde by the way," he said as he sat at the table trying not to make her any more uncomfortable.

"I'm Skylynn; however, most just call me Skye. It's nice to properly meet you Clyde," she said as she gave a small bow before leaving to fetch water.

Looking now at the table, the food smelled and looked delicious. It wasn't a fancy meal by any means, but it was quite inviting, nonetheless. It was some sort of stew with a thick broth almost as if it were milk. There were plenty of vegetables and herbs visible within it as well. Beside it were five golden biscuits. The smell alone would make any hungry person's mouth water and Clyde was no exception. He forcibly put the lid on top of the bowl and decided it would be rude if he ate before anyone else.

Shortly after, Skye came back with the pitcher of water and quickly poured 3 large cups full and set them on the table.

"Do you not like stew? I can make you something else if you like," said Skye in a kind voice.

"No, no, I just figured It would be better to wait for everyone to get here. I hear a meal always tastes best with good company," Clyde said with a smile.

"I see. I never thought about that. I suppose I do enjoy my meal better when Skaald's home," she said as she sat down at the table to the left of Clyde.

Luckily, the silence was broken by Skaald opening the door.

"Well, I'm surprised you waited on me. The smell alone is starving me. Let's eat," said Skaald as he opened the pot and served the portions to Clyde and Skye before sitting down.

The stew was very filling and delicious even with just a small amount of meat. There was still half a pot left when Skye sealed the wooden lid on top and set it near the stove, probably to preserve it for tomorrow's meal.

"So, have you thought of any new questions you'd like to ask. You had better ask them now rather than find yourself in a bind later," pressured Skaald.

"W... well, if it's not rude of me to ask, what race is your wife? I've just never seen anything like her before," Clyde asked reluctantly.

"So, you've never seen a Lizardian before," asked Skye before Skaald could.

"I'm fortunate that you're the first."

"So that's why you stared at me for so long," Skye said, seemingly teasing Clyde. "My people were the first settlers of this land before the Humans, Elves, and Dwarves arrived and eventually dwindled us down to the few of us that's left. There's three main tribes of Lizardians left these days. You have the Amphibious swamp dwellers far to the west in the Great Forest Swamp and then you have the Frozen Tundra clan far to the north and finally my tribe of wanderers. Although we are called wanderers, many of my tribe have settled to the southeast close to the coast. There are a few lingering stragglers from other clans; unfortunately, there's no telling where any of them are," explained Skye with the look of nostalgia in her eyes.

"How long ago did the other races begin expanding here?"

"Hmm. I'd say it's been at least three and a half centuries now since they settled here."

"Were you there when it happened," asked Clyde as his curiosity peaked.

"Yes, I was still quite young back then so most of those memories were told to me by my mother," said Skye as she retrieved a small cask from one of the cupboards. She then removed the cork and poured three cups full of the liquid before offering one to Clyde.

"Ahh, I see it's hard for you to understand," added Skaald as he grabbed his cup and took a big drink before continuing.

"Lizardians live to be around six to seven centuries old. I forgot that you only understand Human lifespans. Just for reference, Dwarves and Elves have similarly long lives."

"I see. I apologize if I was being rude questioning your age Mrs. Skye," said Clyde as he took a testing sip of the mysterious sweet-smelling liquid.

"Oh, I don't mind at all. Unlike you Humans, my people are quite prideful of their age the older we get. As a matter of fact, you can guess how many centuries old a Lizardian is by the color of our tails," Skye explained as she turned around showing her tail off.

"The darker one's tail is compared to the scales on the rest of our body is the easiest way to guess. If it's black, they're closer to seven and if it's closer to my natural complexion, they'll be closer to two centuries old. Any younger than that, their tail won't be fully developed." After Skye finished explaining, she realized her dress was lifted as she was showing her tail, and her face glowed a bright purple as she hid it back under her dress and sat back down at the table quietly.

"Ha, ha, ha, you got carried away didn't you love," laughed Skaald deeply as he took another drink.

The drink in question was a type of honey-sweetened mead. It wasn't a very strong alcohol, but it was quite a refreshing addition to the conversation.

"Dwarves show their ages in their beards and elves by their ears. Nothing too complicated but if you'd like, I'll even let you touch mine! Ha, ha, ha," said Skaald, teasing Skye.

"He shouldn't have to. He can tell without looking that I'm more respectable between us," Skye jabbed back

"I appreciate all the information you've both shared. It has helped me understand so much more. If it's not too much trouble, could I ask a few other questions to help me understand more," asked Clyde, trying to change the subject to something more beneficial.

"Please go ahead," said Skye as she refilled Skaald and Clyde's cups with the sweet mead.

"Can you explain the currency you mentioned earlier, Skaald? That should be the first thing I need to figure out before I make too many decisions."

"Mmm, that's a simple enough question. Let me get some different kinds here," Skaald said as he went and grabbed a lockbox from another cupboard.

Skaald produced four different coins and placed them in front of Clyde.

"The simplest way is to start with the least valued one here," said Skaald as he pointed to the worn brownish-green coin.

"This is a copper neros. It takes about three to purchase a piece of day-old bread and a cup of water. Next, you have the iron neros which is equal to about eight copper ones. It's not a commonly used coin due to its value being odd as well as iron being more valuable as a resource than a currency. Then you've got the silver neros which is worth about twenty-one coppers. You can live comfortably for a week off of one silver neros. Finally, you have the golden neros right here. It's not very commonly used around here due to it being worth about four silvers. Now, don't take these values to heart because the value changes based on a few factors. Mainly the only ones you need to worry about would be location as well as time. The values exchange differently depending on how close you are to the capital of the kingdom. As far as time, that's just something you'll have to get a feel for." After Skaald finished his expiration, he placed the coins back into his lockbox and put it back into its cupboard.

"I understand why you were so surprised by my counter offer now... but is that exoskeleton really worth five gold," asked Clyde as he helped Skye clean the table.

"Honestly, as hard as it is to get them, its value would be closer to eight gold... maybe ten to the right person," Skaald explained as Clyde followed him back to the forge after Skye shewed them out of the kitchen.

"Is that the only reason they're valuable?"

"Well, the fact that they are rare is one thing for sure but the value I referred to was the crafting value of it. It is very useful in reinforcing armor. Speaking of which, I'd say your armor needs some fixing after your fight with that Gex." Skaald then began shoveling some coal and breathing life into the forge.

"Yea, that's what I was going to work on next. It seems as though I'm gonna need my armor in better shape if I'm gonna do any traveling," said Clyde as he picked up his scarred breastplate off the ground.

"Hmmm... why don't I show you how to combine it with your armor? Bring it over here. It's easier than you might think," Skaald said as he threw the Gex shell on the anvil.

"But that's my payment for staying here. I'll just use some of your scrap to fix it."

"You're not putting me out anything so don't worry about it. Besides, you'll be the first one other than me that knows how to put these carcasses to use that I know of," said Skaald as he broke the shell in half.

"Well, if you insist. I suppose I can't stop you..." Clyde said, finally giving in.

They worked throughout the night as Skaald taught Clyde some Dwarven forging techniques as well as the ones he came up with to fuse the Gex shell to steel. They repaired and reinforced Clyde's armor and Clyde got a chance to learn how to do everything he used to do just with primitive equipment.

A few days later, Skaald introduced Clyde to his connections within the town as well as bought

Clyde a thin but durable cloak to show off how his connections worked to acquire whatever you need. Clyde spent the next few weeks doing odd jobs and getting familiar with the town until he decided on what he was going to do. He made up his mind nearing the end of his first month in this new world just as he was beginning to grasp how to read not only the Common tongue but some Dwarvish as well.

"So, you've decided what you're gonna start doing, eh? Well, let's hear it," said Skaald across the table eating the hard bread from yesterday by dipping it in water.

"Yes, I'm gonna travel through No Man's Land to reach the northern town." And as soon as the words left Clyde's mouth, he heard a crash as Skye dropped her clay pitcher on the ground out of shock.

"What are you thinking," Skye shouted angrily, which startled Clyde as it wasn't usual for her to burst out.

"Calm down. Let's hear if the boy has any sense before you beat it into him," Skaald said with a harsh tone.

Clyde readjusted his posture before beginning his explanation.

"My plan is simple. I'm not just gonna jump right in and expect that I'm gonna make it without preparing myself first. I plan on going out a few days at a time to see if I can scout out a decent path as well as study the hunting patterns of the Gex and whatever else might be there. After I feel I've prepared enough, I'll set out for the town to the north and make myself a safe route through No Man's Land," explained Clyde hoping that it satisfied Skye's worry.

"There's still no guarantee you won't be killed even after a day's travel into that place! I haven't been teaching you just for you to go off and die like a fool," shouted Skye as her tail was thrashing about angrily behind her.

After she was out of either things to say or breath to shout at them, she stormed out of the kitchen leaving Clyde and Skaald sitting quietly with one another.

"Well, that's the most upset she's been in a decade.... It seems as though she's taken quite a liking to you, boy. Don't take her words to heart. She just doesn't want to see you get yourself killed," explained Skaald, breaking the rough silence.

"Well, I don't want to make her worry but if I'm gonna be able to survive out in the world, I'm gonna have to take this chance and learn how to overcome this before I can decide what I plan to do in this world," Clyde explained.

"Well, I'll help you as much as I can. Also, Skye is probably gonna give you the cold shoulder until you come back safely," said Skaald before finishing the remainder of his bread followed quickly by the rest of his water.

"Then I'll be sure to come back then," said Clyde confidently.

Chapter 2: Making Goals Realities

Within the next few weeks, Clyde made his preparations to venture into No Man's Land. As far as equipment, Skaald helped him repair and make adjustments to his armor making it lighter and more convenient and comfortable to wear for long periods of time. The helmet was similar to a Renaissance era closed helmet with bars instead of slits on the visor for better visibility. The breastplate was nothing too eccentric but was shortened trading protection for convenience so Clyde could easily bend and maneuver while his midsection simply had leather to offer a small amount of protection. He only wore leather gloves and vambraces made from the remainder of the Gex shell due to it being lighter but just as strong as steel ones. He also used a Gex shell for his greaves and cuisse for the same reason. As for footwear, he was already wearing leather steel toed boots when he woke up so they would work until he wore them out. He used a mixture including beeswax and a few other things to make his armor more weather resistant and give it a dark almost black like color. After he put his leather backpack on filled with his waterskin and other supplies he covered himself with his dark worn cloak that Skaald had bought him, and he was ready to go.

Clyde left before the sun or anyone in the house even rose to start the day. He noticed that his pack had been moved since the previous day but nonetheless he was off. Following the relative path he used to get to the village, he began his journey into No Man's Land.

Throughout the first day, he was simply looking for Gex tracks that were a day old or fresher. As he looked, he was also memorizing everything within sight looking for used paths or an easier path to travel towards the town in the north. After about a half a day's travel, Clyde found the tracks he was searching for. They looked very fresh, possibly from that night which made Clyde feel a bit uncomfortable seeing that it was at least five sets of tracks, possibly six. The tracks were heading northwest, possibly in a large field barely visible to Clyde. The field in question was very large and seemed easy to get to but it had two large cliffs on either side that plateaued and then raised to a ridge similar to the one Clyde currently stood on.

I wonder if that is their hunting grounds, questioned Clyde to himself deciding on what he should do.

Clyde wanted to go investigate the field but unfortunately based on the distance it would take almost the rest of the day just to make it to the field. The only problem was that Clyde said he would only take day trips until he got used to the terrain and to make Skye happy. Unfortunately for Skye, Clyde's curiosity won, and he ventured onward. He stayed with the tracks for a while to confirm that they were for sure going to the field in question. When he followed the tracks for about four hours, he decided to head to one of the plateaus that overlooked the field.

Once he reached the plateau after a tedious climb, the travel was much easier; the ground was almost completely flat with only large borders scattered about until it began to incline again towards another ridge. The view was incredible looking down towards the field as the sun was just beginning to set. Clyde walked for about another hour along the cliff edge looking down into the field searching for any sign of Gex or other life. Once he was about halfway, he saw movement in the field heading towards the way he thought the Gex had come into the field and when they got closer it was indeed the Gex pack. They were chasing what looked to be a herd of rhinoceros-like creatures that were as fast or possibly faster than a horse. The Gex were having trouble catching them; however, at the same time, it looked as if they were herding them. Clyde sat and watched them as the sun was slowly setting and visibility was getting lower and lower. Just before it was too dark to watch them, Clyde witnessed just how intelligent the Gex were. They were indeed herding their prey into an ambush of three or four other Gex hiding in the tall grass which when the beast ran by, they jumped out and successfully killed a few of them. It had gotten too dark to be able to count how many and, at that, Clyde decided it was well past time for himself to have something to eat. Clyde made his way to one of the large boulders that had an overhang large enough to sit under and Clyde unlatched his pack and began to dig out his rations. As Clyde opened his pouch of food, to his surprise there was far more than he packed the previous day along with a piece of parchment in between a meat pie and a small loaf of rye bread. After Clyde hastily retrieved the meat pie and began eating the unexpected treat of a meal, he read the contents of the parchment before it was too dark to do so.

"Just in case something were to happen and you stayed longer than you promised, I made you something to last more than a day. However, don't get the idea that I'm still not angry with you. I just want to make sure you keep your promise. Also, I found you a book with some more complex words for you to continue your studies."

As Clyde read the hastily written letter, he couldn't help but smile to himself thinking just how lucky he was to find such kind people to help him. Soon after he finished his meat pie, the sun had fully set and at the current time of year, winter was vastly approaching meaning nights were quite cold. Apparently from what Skaald explained, the only thing winter brings is the cold and very little snow because it's a dry climate with little precipitation regardless so fortunately the season won't affect travel. The only problem was that building a fire was just asking to be a target, but Clyde was well prepared to live without it. Instead, Clyde draped his cloak over himself and lit a small candle which he placed under his cloak in between his legs which in turn heated Clyde's body nicely. There was one drawback to this which was the cost of candles, which were fairly expensive in this region costing half of a silver neros a piece. Clyde did try to conserve them though; as once he was warm, he put out the candle which allowed him to get about three good uses out of one. Although after Clyde put out the candle, he intended to stay awake throughout the night. Unfortunately, he must have dozed off soon after getting warm because the next thing he noticed was the sun waking him up the next morning.

"I'm gonna run out of luck if I keep doing things like this," Clyde said to himself as he roused himself awake, checking the surrounding area to make sure he was safely alone.

Clyde soon gathered himself and prepared for the day's journey. After he was ready to set out, he scanned the field looking for any sign of Gex or the other creature. To his surprise, where the Gex had ambushed their prey, they were in fact still there enjoying their kill. Since there was plenty of light, Clyde could accurately count that they killed five of the beasts which seems to be able to last the Gex for possibly a few days. Clyde observed for a while longer, noticing that only a few at a time would eat while the rest seemed to be lookouts for any sort of danger or possibly more prey, and after an hour or so they rotated, proving that they had some sort of intelligence. Clyde took one last scan of the field and finally spotted the herd of prey at the far edge of the field as if they were migrating to another area away from the Gex.

"Maybe the Gex follow the herd after they move which is why anyone traveling through here becomes an easy meal," Clyde explained to himself as he began walking back towards the town.

Clyde decided to try making a new path to the town to make it easier to get to the plateaus. If his suspicion was right about the Gex and prey migrating, this would be an easy passage towards the northern town.

Surprisingly, it took almost half a day off the trip and Clyde ended up on the side of town that had the forge which was quite convenient. As Clyde approached the door, he paused as he was unsure how to approach Skye as she would probably be upset with him. As he pondered on whether or not it was worth going inside, a familiar voice snapped Clyde back to reality.

"Well, it looks like you made it back in one piece," said Skaald as he patted Clyde roughly on the back.

"Yea... my curiosity got the better of me," explained Clyde.

"You'd better come up with a better excuse than that. She's been up all night worrying about you.... I'd say you're in for a lecture or two," said Skaald pushing Clyde closer toward the door.

Clyde swallowed his uncertainty and opened the door, instantly meeting the gaze of Skye as he walked through, unable to make eye contact with her. Before he could fully enter the house, she seemingly pounced toward Clyde unexpectedly. She grabbed his shoulders firmly with her strong grip and claws digging into his cloak making the situation unavoidable. Clyde had lost what little composure he had and simply accepted whatever she was going to do or say; but to Clyde's surprise, the only thing she did was quietly check him over from head to toe and smelled him all over similar to what a dog would do for an uncomfortable few seconds. When she was seemingly satisfied, she looked into Clyde's eyes and sighed a sigh of relief.

"You don't smell like you had any trouble on your way so explain why you're late," said Skye in a soft but serious tone.

"W... well, I found some fresh Gex tracks, so I decided to follow them to see..."

"Were you looking to get yourself killed," interjected Skye as her tone turned to anger quicker than Clyde anticipated.

"I was keeping my distance. I had no intentions of..." Clyde was interrupted by a sudden slap across his face. The slap itself didn't hurt because it seemed that Skye was just as surprised by what she did as Clyde was.

She took a step back and began walking away but was stopped by Clyde's next words.

"I'm sorry I made you worry... but thank you for the extra food. I enjoyed it," Clyde said, giving her a sincere smile out of the amusement of her overreaction.

"W... well, don't get used to it... you'd best learn not to make me angry," she said as her face began to turn purple out of embarrassment before she went into the kitchen.

Clyde and Skaald stood in silence for a bit before Skaald finally broke the tension.

"Ahh, that's right. Darren at the general store is looking for you. He said the supplies you ordered are in," Skaald said as he walked over and opened the door to the forge room.

"Also, the wife can be quite emotional and hardheaded at times when she cares about something so try not to take that scolding to heart you hear," said Skaald standing in the doorway.

"Right... Well, hopefully I don't keep upsetting her. I should be back a bit after dark. I'm gonna head on over to Darren's," Clyde said as he headed off to the general store.

Over the past few weeks, Clyde became accustomed to using the back alleys rather than the streets so Clyde could avoid being social. Although if it came down to it, he could pretend to be quite charismatic and outgoing as he needed but he preferred to keep his social interactions to a minimum. The shopkeeper in question was one of the few that Clyde enjoyed talking to. Not only were they similar in age but Clyde had sort of an admiration for Darren. He had a family and a well-rounded personality about him and also was rather young to own and run his own shop. As a matter of fact, most of the odd jobs and such Clyde had been doing was for Darren and he paid quite well so he wasn't just barely managing his little town shop, he seemed to be doing quite well for himself.

Once Clyde came to the rear entrance of the shop, he could hear a commotion coming from within. It didn't seem hostile so Clyde simply entered as quietly as he could so he didn't disturb anyone. He got within earshot of the conversation and although he thought he shouldn't, he decided to eavesdrop.

"I'm sorry they didn't send any of the medicine you ordered on this shipment. They must have had trouble getting it this time of year," Darren's muffled voice echoed.

"What do you mean they didn't send it!!! They were short the past two times and I paid almost double for it," shot an old man's voice filled with anger.

"I'll check once more but there's no record of it even being on the shipment," said Darren as he entered the back room where Clyde was.

"Oh, look who survived the wrath of the angry lizard. She didn't let you go unscathed I see," said Darren as he looked at Clyde's face

When Clyde put his hand to his cheek to inspect what Darren meant, he found that his face had been cut. More than likely by Skye's claws which explained why she looked so shocked. Clyde took a rag on the table and cleaned the small amount of blood on his face before following Darren into his stockroom.

The room was well organized but only in Darren's mind. It looked neat and tidy; however, only Darren knew where to find anything he was looking for. Shelves went almost to the ceiling, and they were arranged in a maze-like pattern across the large room. Darren kept the valuables in very different areas of the room that were either difficult to find or hidden in something that wasn't very valuable. He said it was to keep robbers from making a quick score which was believable, but Clyde just assumed he liked the general chaos of the room.

"Sigh.... No, there's definitely none of that medicine here..." Darren said as he rummaged through some small chests.

"What kind of medicine is it," asked Clyde as he was rummaging through a random chest full of trinkets.

"It's some sort of experimental stuff the Elven college down south was experimenting with from what I've heard. Unfortunately, they are also known to drop their experiments without any warning to anyone else involved," explained Darren as he emerged from the rear of the storeroom.

"So, why does the old man need it so badly," Clyde asked as he shoved the trinkets back in the box as Darren turned the corner.

"I need it for my granddaughter," came an irritated voice from the doorway.

Clyde turned toward the old man. Figuring curiosity had brought him this far, why not continue?

"So, what's the matter with your granddaughter to need to rely on some special medicine?"

"She has something called Manalocitis or that's at least what the doctor that used to come to the village called it," said the old man with careful wording.

"Could this doctor treat whatever it is," asked Clyde as they all went back toward the front of the store.

"Apparently when he went to the town to the north a few years ago no one has been able to contact him." interjected Darren as he was preparing to close the shop.

"How serious is this sickness to your granddaughter's health," asked Clyde, almost regretting getting involved.

"If left like she is, I don't see her lasting more than a month," said the old man as his voice began to shake.

"So, tell me just how much you are willing to pay for someone to find this doctor of yours," asked Clyde as he watched the old man's expression turn from sadness to distaste.

"I... I'll pay whatever I can afford so long as she gets to grow up," said the old man in an almost angry tone.

"Sounds worth my while... So how do I recognize this doctor of yours? A name or any distinct features that you know about?"

"I believe they called him Dr. Montgomery. As far as a feature, I remember he had a false eye that wasn't the same color as his real one," the old man said, straining his memory.

"I'll see what I can do. I'll set out in the morning, old man," Clyde said as he opened the door to let the old man out of the shop.

After Clyde shut the door behind him, he heard Darren chuckling softly to himself.

"So, our stray is nothing but a big softie now isn't he," said Darren, unable to keep a straight face.

"Soft or not, it gives me a good reason to head north," said Clyde trying to stay cold.

"If you're not careful, Skye's gonna end up hurting you worse than a Gex ever could," Darren said, pointing toward Clyde's face as he lit an oil lamp with a spark of magic.

"Well, luckily you've got what I asked for right," asked Clyde as he watched Darren light another lamp.

"Yea, let me see if it all came in...." He took a sheet of parchment laying on the table and held it near the lamp before continuing.

"Six and five eighths' pounds of salt, a seasoned four-foot ash wood rod, six candles, and last but not least, a large apron with blue flowers on it." As

Darren finished the list, he looked up at Clyde and continued.

"So as agreed for the equivalent of twelve gold and three silvers worth of work, here is your order. I gift wrapped your suck up gift on the house," finished Darren followed with a mischievous smile.

"Unfortunately, it's going to be closer to a peace offering. I don't see her taking too well of me going right back into No Man's Land."

"So, you're not taking the loop around," asked Darren.

"No, from what I understand, if you make good time it takes over a month one way if you take the safe route around No Man's Land. But if the maps I've read are correct on the distance, it should take no more than seven or eight days to go straight through if you account for detours and such," explained Clyde packing his things to prepare to leave.

"Well, try to make it back in one piece... It's hard to make a dead man buy you a drink," said Darren blowing out one of the lamps.

"Who said I owe you a drink," shot Clyde as he heaved his large pack into one of Darren's empty wheelbarrows.

"Well, for one, finding that much salt this close to winter and lastly, giving you a job," shot Darren closing the door on Clyde ending the meaningless conversation.

Clyde didn't waste any time as he made his route through the back alleys to the forge. As he entered through the side door straight to the forge, Skaald was there tending the fire to the forge.

"I figured you might need to touch up your equipment but first you'd better go eat a bite before she gives me a matching face," said Skaald laughingly.

Clyde nodded and unpacked his things and prepared his gift before going into the kitchen. As soon as he walked in, he noticed Skye gave him a glance then turned away towards the stove as if she were preparing the food again. Clyde took the opportunity to grab a bowl full of the stew that was still quite warm on the table hiding his gift for afterwards. After a few moments of awkward silence and Clyde finished his stew, Skye finally turned around and prepared to speak.

"I... I... I didn't mean to be so upset at you. I just..." she paused as if trying to remember an apology she rehearsed but before she could continue, Clyde interrupted.

"I appreciate that you've taken me under your wing as you have and that I'm worth worrying about. Besides, I should be the one apologizing because I'm about to do something far more dangerous," said Clyde, waiting for a response from the now more flustered Skye.

"What do you mean, more dangerous," she said quietly.

"Apparently there's a sick little girl in town that needs some miracle doctor from the northern town. And she needs him within a month's time."

"The granddaughter of the Hawkford family... don't tell me you're the one going," said Skye, seemingly knowing the girl's situation.

"I'm heading out in the morning... I'm sorry, but I feel like it's worth trying," shrugged Clyde

"Sigh... I'll make your rations... If you find this doctor or not, I expect to see you back," exasperated Skye.

Clyde took an involuntary sigh of relief and then set the package on the table. Skye turned around and walked over curiously.

"I got you a gift for being so kind to me these past few weeks, but you're not allowed to open it until after I leave tomorrow," explained Clyde, hoping to dodge whatever emotions she'll undoubtedly go through whilst opening a present.

"Well, I appreciate the gesture, but this is unnecessary," she said as her gaze never left the brown packaging, and her tail seemingly swished about more frequently than normal.

"It's not much so don't be too disappointed when you open it," said Clyde as he left the kitchen heading towards the forge room.

Clyde and Skaald spent the majority of the night tweaking his equipment and making a short spear out of the wooden rod and the tip of the blade of the Gex arm Clyde brought. He specifically made it short but balanced so he could easily maneuver it with one hand and be capable of killing a Gex easier than with a sword.

With dawn fast approaching and Clyde's new spear easily attached to his pack full of provisions under his cloak, he was ready to set out. Using his newly discovered path, he made easy time going back to his previous vantage point. Although he looked along the way, he couldn't find any fresh tracks. Hopefully this was a good sign, but Clyde was still quite alert. At the end of the first day, he was close to the far edge of the valley he was watching a hunt in just the other day. He scanned it off and on as he walked but there was no sign of the Gex or the other creature at all. So, Clyde finally decided on a place to camp and concluded his first day. Clyde woke up unscathed at sunrise of the second day. After quickly collecting himself, he climbed down the new side of the plateau and began heading north. He avoided taking the obvious well-traveled path of the Gex and other wildlife and chose to follow it from a distance since it was going in the same direction he needed to go. The next two days were relatively uneventful as Clyde simply followed the path which led to the various watering holes throughout the journey. On the fourth day, Clyde came to a T in the path. There seemed to be an older set of tracks heading west and much fresher tracks following the east path wrapping around from what Clyde could tell was various valleys and hills off into the distance. There were remnants of a few carcasses where the Gex must have fed but other than that, there wasn't any real reason Clyde could find that they wouldn't continue north. Despite Clyde's curiosity, he decided to leave the trail altogether and continued travelling north.

Before dusk had properly set in and Clyde had found himself on another sort or plateau, he found the possible reason the trails split as they did. He walked to the edge of what seemed to be a large crack in the ground that was too wide to jump and far too deep to simply climb down and cross. At the bottom was a fast-flowing river crashing violently down below causing interesting echoes up the walls. Clyde remembered from the maps he looked at that this was the only marked river in No Man's Land, and it had been appropriately called The Death's Whisper due to the ominous sounds the echoes made. As it was getting too dark to find a solution to cross, Clyde decided to wait until morning. After a questionable night of sleep, Clyde was searching for a solution to his problem. He walked along the edge searching for something he could work with and found a large tree on the wrong side of the river. After a bit more searching and consideration, that was the only relevant option Clyde had so he retrieved the rope he had in his bag and attached it to his kukri to use as a sort of grapple. After a few attempts, Clyde managed to snag the rope to one of the tree branches which seemed able to hold Clyde's weight. After a bit more reconsidering, Clyde finally decided to go for it and successfully swung to the other side of the ravine.

After Clyde retrieved his things, he made note of where the tree was for the return trip and continued north. The remainder of the trip was rather easy on Clyde as he topped the last ridge and finally saw the port town of Clydesdoor. The breeze brought the salty scent of the bay that the town was molded to. It was hard to call it a town as it was even surrounded with a sturdy wall and far larger than the town Clyde just came from. As he approached the town, he noticed that there was a well-traveled road that seemed to go far to the west leading right to the town, so Clyde began following it. As he got closer, he came upon a small shack with some armed guards manning it.

"Halt... state your business traveler," stated one of the guards.

"I'm here on a job," said Clyde vaguely.

"What kind of job... Do you have any documentation," asked the guard, irritated.

"I need to deliver a message is all, possibly a little shopping afterwards if it's not too much trouble."

"Right... you'll have to pay the toll to enter Clydesdoor then," said the guard as he pulled a logbook of sorts out.

"How much is it then," asked Clyde as he reached for his coin pouch.

"Two silver Neros," said the guard as he was writing with a charcoal stick.

Clyde reluctantly paid the tax and was let through the checkpoint without much more issue and continued past the gate into the large town. This town was far more active and bustling than the last one and the smells and sights were simply overwhelming. Clyde wandered about for a bit before finally finding a place to start asking questions. Clyde found himself in a small inn that seemed rather cheap. The sign was hanging on by only one brace and the door was barely on the hinges when Clyde opened it. The place seemed quite empty except for one elderly man sitting by the fire.

"Excuse me, is this an inn," Clyde asked the old man.

The old man opened his eyes and carefully examined Clyde before sitting up in his chair. He took a long drink of whatever was in his cask and made eye contact with Clyde.

"Two copper for one night, four copper for three..." said the old man as he leaned back waiting for Clyde's response.

Clyde handed the old man four copper Neros and sat down in the chair across from the old man.

"How about one night and some questions," asked Clyde.

The old man carefully examined the coins he received and simply nodded before he put them away. Clyde assumes that was a yes and prepared to ask his question.

"I'm looking for a man with a mismatched false eye... He may call himself some sort of doctor. Do you have any idea where I could start looking for him," Clyde asked as he got up and stoked the fire for the old man.

There was silence while Clyde tended the fire as the old man simply watched, and he didn't say anything until Clyde sat back down.

"There's a cheap place to drink called the silver bow down towards the docks.... My granddaughter knows a lot of people... she's the barkeep," said the old man before he seemingly fell asleep.

Clyde only sat for a short while longer before heading out to this silver bow bar. It wasn't very difficult to find and seemed to be quite the busy little bar. As Clyde approached the entrance, he was pushed out of the way by some young men practically carrying an older, far drunker man out of the bar. After they started down the street,

Clyde made it into the bar and made his way to the counter. The place was quite loud with everyone talking and a small band playing some kind of music; the atmosphere was surprisingly inviting from what Clyde could tell. Soon after Clyde had waited at the bar, a stunning young bartender came over and prepared to serve Clyde.

"What can I get you started on tonight," said the bartender as she started cleaning a glass.

"How about a cold glass of information," said Clyde smiling as he stacked a few pieces of copper on the table.

The bartender's smile didn't last as she grabbed the coins and poured a glass of what Clyde could only guess was some poor grog.

"Make it quick. I've got customers to keep drunk," she said coldly.

"I'm looking for a man that goes by the name Montgomery. He's got a noticeably false eye as well," said Clyde before drinking the foul-tasting grog.

"Huh, that poor drunk has a lot of punks after him tonight. He was with the lot that left right before you came in and wasted my time. You'd best find whatever alley they took him to if you want to see the poor fella breathing again," she said, taking Clyde's now empty glass and wiping it clean.

"Thanks, next time I hope to be a customer," said Clyde as he left a silver piece on the counter before rushing out the door.

He looked around the street in the direction they were heading, and he saw what could pass for an alleyway not too far from the bar. As he walked closer, he could hear the sound of talking and laughing. As he peeked around the corner, he saw the same four guys surrounding a man on his knees being held up by the collar. The one holding him was the loudest asking him something about something before pummeling the fellow again. Clyde thought for a second if it was worth breaking up, but the thoughts of the sick little girl gave him the motivation to get involved and after a sigh of resentment, he began confidently strolling down the alley.

"So, tell me what's so funny now... huh, I can't hear you." said the guy holding and beating the guy on his knees.

"Hey, someone's coming," alerted one of the others.

At this distance, Clyde got the assumption that these punks acted and sounded like they were young, possibly in their early twenties if they were human. So, he figured that being aggressive might be the easiest way to make them stop beating on his delivery. As he was thinking this, the supposed leader of the group dropped the doctor and walked out to confront Clyde.

"Who do you think you are punk... some kinda hero that saves drunks like this," asked the boy looking as tough as he could.

"Ha, ha, sorry to disappoint but im nowhere close to being a hero... especially not with what I'm probably about to do to you," said Clyde as he got closer to the young man, seeing that this one was in fact human.

"You know that we're in the Corvix guild, right," asked the lad as the other three took a step closer.

"In all honesty, I couldn't care less... but I'll be nice. You guys can either walk away and leave my buddy over there with me or we can do this the hard way," said Clyde as he reached through his cloak grabbing the clasp that held it together.

The punk didn't even give an answer before he began to rear back for a punch. Unfortunately for him, Clyde was already prepared for this fight as he unlatched his cloak. Before the cloak fell to the ground, the first strike went to Clyde as he unrelentingly kicked the poor lad in the scrotum dropping him to the ground in pain. Clyde instantly had to jump back as a bolt of fire came flying toward him from one of the others.

A magic user is a problem I need to deal with next, thought Clyde as he dodged another fire bolt.

Immediately, one of the others came flying above Clyde trying to land an axe kick. Clyde dodged just for them to land he moved too quickly and threw a quick punch toward Clyde. Clyde deflected his unfittingly powerful punch and was close and fast enough to jab him right in the throat stunning him enough for Clyde to grab what Clyde assumed was his hair and slam his head against the alley wall. Clyde then sprinted toward the magic user as the last thug got in his way holding some kind of weapon. It was getting darker fast, and Clyde could only make out the outline of the two that remained standing as he prepared to make his next move. Luckily, the mage started casting another fire bolt giving Clyde enough light to move on the guy with a weapon. The man lunged toward Clyde attempting to stab him with the blade and Clyde grabbed the blade tightly with one hand the man's shirt with the other. Clyde, then, pushed the man in the way of the incoming firebolt that came from the magic user. As it hit his back, the fire exploded in all directions before disappearing and Clyde threw the guy to the ground and stomped his arm forcing him to let go of his weapon. As soon as he did, Clyde threw it to the side and quickly closed the gap with the magic user before he could make another fireball and grabbed his shoulder firmly.

"If I were you, I'd take the loss and drag your friends back to that guild of yours while you're still able to stand," Clyde said in-between breaths.

"Y... yea... sh... sure man... whatever you say," said the magic user as he began to take Clyde's advice.

After the two able to stand got the other two on their feet, the loud one turned to Clyde before running off.

"You'll regret doing this when the boss finds out."

After they left, Clyde collected his cloak and walked over to the man just barely conscious and covered in mud.

"I sure hope you're Dr. Montgomery because that's unfortunately gonna be a future problem for me," said Clyde as he tried to help the guy to his feet unsuccessfully.

"I quit being a doctor years ago," muttered the drunk, beaten man.

"Well, that means you're probably who I'm looking for I guess," said Clyde as he just picked the doctor up and started walking back to the inn as the doctor helplessly attempted to fight it.

Once Clyde got back to the inn, he patched up the doctor's mangled face and let him sleep off his drunk. Clyde gave the old inn keeper a few extra coins for all the trouble and Clyde stayed awake for the remainder of the night making sure nothing happened. Fortunately, the night was uneventful, and the doctor woke up at a reasonable hour not expecting to be greeted by Clyde.

"Ugh, my head…. So how much do I owe your boss," said Dr. Montgomery after he realized Clyde was sitting by the window.

"You don't owe me any money, but you do owe me some gratitude for cleaning you off the street," said Clyde, somewhat annoyed at his accusation.

"Well, I'm afraid there's nothing I can give you if you can't already tell," he said straining as he sat up.

"I'm afraid that's not true Dr. Montgomery," Clyde said as he watched for his reaction.

As soon as Clyde said his name, he understandably seemed shocked that a stranger knew his name.

"How do you know me.... I haven't been a doctor for over ten years now," he said as he looked down at his hands.

"There's a town to the south called Strand with a sick girl and the one that hired me sent me after you," said Clyde as he began packing his pack.

"I never agreed that I'm going with you, what are you packing up for," the doctor asked as he crawled out of bed.

Clyde threw him a waterskin before standing up and throwing his pack on.

"I never agreed that you had an option, you sorry excuse of a drunk." Clyde then put his cloak on before opening the door and waited for the doctor.

When the doctor stood up, he simply looked at Clyde for a moment as if he were trying to find a reasonable argument.

"Well, I need to get away from this place anyway. I guess going with you is better than dying here," said the doctor as he accepted Clyde's open-door invitation.

As Clyde said goodbye to the old innkeeper, he and his new companion left the inn only to be met by an unfriendly face. As they walked out into the street, there were four armed men outside waiting for them.

"Well, look who's finally awake. The poor old drunk and his guardian angel," said the one in the most expensive looking gear.

"So, I heard you were picking on some of my green recruits in an alleyway last night... It seems that I'm gonna have to teach someone some common decency," he said as he stepped forward.

Clyde stepped in front of the doctor reaching his hand out to unclasp his cloak while his other hand was ready to draw his sword. He could tell that these men were far more experienced in a fight than the ones last night, so he wasn't liking his odds. He was going to try to talk him down before actually gunning straight for a fight.

"To be fair, I did give them a fair warning to leave before they decided to fight," said Clyde as he carefully watched their body language.

"Oh, did you now... well, that is a bit different than the story I heard and unfortunately for you, I think I believe my men over some low-class mercenary," said the man as he subtly reached for his sword.

Clyde wasn't liking the outcome that played out in his mind, so he thought harder on a peaceful solution.

"Listen, I'm not saying your men are lying but to be fair, I had to stop them from damaging my delivery any more than he is. You know how some customers are about details," said Clyde, boasting his best fake smile.

The man let go of his sword for a moment and closed his eyes for a moment.

"I can see where you're coming from man, but you didn't have to go so hard on my rookies," he said as he crossed his arms.

"Well, it was dark when I found them, so I simply fought on instinct. I couldn't see that they were novices until after I took a few down," explained Clyde as he was still on high alert.

"Sigh... alright. I'll tell ya what... since this is the first time I've seen you in town, I'll let it slide this once. Just so you know, if you cause my men trouble again, I'm not gonna be so tolerant next time." As he said that, the other three men's intensity faded making Clyde feel able to drop his guard a bit.

"I appreciate the pass. I'll be sure to not be as much trouble next time," said Clyde as he withdrew his hand back in his cloak.

"Good to hear, merc... Let's go boys. If I'm late again, I'll never hear the end of it," said the man as he quickly walked off with his guards.

Clyde and the doctor began walking to the exit of the town and passed the checkpoint before they spoke again.

"That was about to be quite the mess... Do you think you could have won against all of them," asked the doctor, trying to keep up with Clyde's pace.

"Honestly, if they actually started a fight with me, I'd probably have found an opportunity to run... maybe one on one I could stand a chance but I'm not stupid enough to say I can take all four," said Clyde as they approached where they were going to leave the road.

"Where are we going, don't tell me we're going through No Man's Land," said the doctor stopping after he realized it.

"Unfortunately, your patient doesn't have the time for us to go around so we're gonna have to take a little risk," said Clyde as he turned towards the doctor and stopped in his tracks.

"You call this a little risk? This is insanity," shouted the doctor in protest.

"Listen, I came through here once already. If you listen to me, hopefully, we will make it in one piece," said Clyde, beginning to get irritated.

The doctor paced back and forth for a moment as he was beginning to reconsider following Clyde.

"Fine, let's go. I'd better make it through here or I'm gonna haunt your arrogant ass," said the doctor as he started walking ahead.

Clyde shrugged the comment off, and they went on their way. When they got to Death's Whisper,

Clyde came prepared with an ax he bought before they left town and chopped the lonesome tree down over the ravine so they could easily cross. They successfully made it to the divided paths and began following them back to what Clyde explained was the Plateau Valley. When they made it there, Clyde and the doctor had to stop midday and hide. There was a herd of those large creatures being hunted on the plateau's ledges instead of in the field below and Clyde had failed to see them in time to avoid it. Clyde and the doctor took refuge in a nearby shallow cave they found, and Clyde made a few traps at the entrance to slow any intruders down. The next leg of the journey was not going to be a cake walk.

"I'm gonna go see if I can find us a way out of here," said Clyde as the morning sun penetrated the cave.

"Try not to die," said the doctor as he was finishing up the breakfast Clyde gave him.

Clyde quietly left the cave and began scouting around the plateau. He soon came across the quiet herd of the Gex' prey just grazing quietly. They seemed like any other herd of grazing animals Clyde had known by just the way they were built they seemed almost as dangerous as the Gex. Clyde slipped away from the herd and found a small path with a vantage point so he could figure his situation out. Clyde finally found the Gex who were behind them feeding on their kill from yesterday. From what Clyde could see, the path he took to get to where he was would lead them safely to the other side of the plateau.

"Alright, I've got a path mapped out but until we get away from the herd of prey out there, we have to be quiet," Clyde explained when he got back to the cave.

"You're the boss, just don't get us killed," said the doctor as he handed Clyde his pack and waterskin.

They left the cave and carefully followed the route Clyde had made out and by the end of the day, they were climbing down the plateau. Luckily, they didn't encounter any more trouble on the way to Strand. Once finally in the safety of the town, Clyde took the doctor to Darren who took them to the little girl's home. From what the doctor later explained to Clyde, the girl had been born with a disease that was pumping mana into her bloodstream, effectively poisoning her. After a few operations, she was successfully recovering.

"So, why did you quit being a doctor? You're obviously good at it," asked Clyde as he was sharing a drink with the doctor and Darren,

"I lost a patient I was caring for and it just broke me. I never thought I'd pick up a scalpel again but here we are," said the doctor as he took a big swig of his drink.

"You're lucky you're here from what you guys told me. I can't believe you got on bad terms with the Corvix guild Clyde... I hear they're a pretty tough guild that works as bodyguards against pirates," said Darren as he finished his bottle.

"If I had a choice, I would have kept a low profile... Unfortunately, I had to do something, or we wouldn't have much of a doctor left," said Clyde

"Well, whatever I said to them to make em so upset I can't remember for the life of me, but it all worked out," said the doctor, seemingly falling asleep over his mead.

"So, how much are you getting paid for your brave little journey across No Man's Land," asked Darren, leaning towards Clyde from across the table.

"I haven't really discussed it with the old man. I'll let him have some time to calm down before we work something out," said Clyde as he finished his drink and got up.

"You're heading out already? We've got plenty of mead in stock," said Darren as he pointed to the shelf of jugs.

"I'd better not stay out any later. I heard from Skaald that Skye is making something special for dinner. If I miss it, I won't be fed properly for a month," said Clyde as he headed out the door leaving Darren with his drunken guest.

Chapter 3: Living the New Life

Clyde finally made it to his newfound home after a long and exciting journey. As he approached the large one-story house, he could smell the alluring aroma of the meal Skye must be preparing. Clyde thought to himself, *Just how long has it been since I've come home to something like this."* His mind wandered to the past. He couldn't help but stop just before entering the doorway as Clyde's heart began to ache from pleasant memories of coming home to his father's smiling face questioning him about his day even though there was never anything new to tell him. Clyde couldn't help but feel he never did enough for his father and wondered if this was possibly the second chance he never could have had. Then his mind began to ask why Skye and Skaald took him in like they did without so much as a second thought.

"Boy, if you keep blocking the door, we're both gonna be late for dinner," said Skaald as he firmly put his hand on Clyde's shoulder startling Clyde back to reality.

"R... right," said Clyde as he fumbled to open the door.

"Is there something bothering you," asked Skaald as he picked up a large sack of something before following Clyde inside.

"Well, honestly I was curious as to what made you two take me in like this... I honestly don't deserve this much kindness," said Clyde, not expecting a real answer.

Skaald gave Clyde a side glance as the question was stated. He then stopped and closed his eyes before opening the door to the forge.

"Honestly, I was just going to hold you up to your deal and send you on your way after a few days.... until Skye really took a liking to you, boy. And I hope it goes without saying that you grew on me as well," said Skaald as he opened the door to the forge and beckoned Clyde to follow him.

After Clyde closed the door behind him, Skaald continued, after setting the sack in the corner of the room.

"Skye likes people. There's no doubt about that; except for when it comes to you. I believe that she thinks of you a bit differently. I think, in her eyes, she sees you in a way that she wants to nourish and see grow," said Skaald as he was cleaning his working area seemingly to avoid acknowledging the strangeness of the conversation.

"Nourish," questioned Clyde.

"To put it plainly, if I know anything about my wife, she sees you as an adopted son."

"What? Why me?"

"Well, I can't really answer that. You'll have to ask her. What I can tell you is that she's never had a child of her own even before I ever met her. She said that she'd always dreamed of having children but was, for some reason or another, unable to. So, between me and you boy, if she accepts you as one of her own, I suppose I can as well," said Skaald as he placed his hand again on Clyde's shoulder.

Clyde couldn't help but be happy with Skaald's explanation as he smiled.

"I... I want you to know that you two have helped me far more than you know, and although I don't deserve it, I'm glad that you have accepted me," said Clyde before Skaald grabbed his shirt and pushed him toward the door.

"You'd best get in there before she gets upset with you. She's spent all day preparing this meal."

"Right," said Clyde as he left the forge and began towards the kitchen.

Clyde quietly opened the door and walked through. He saw Skye, who hadn't noticed him yet as she was preparing dinner. He noticed that she was wearing the apron Clyde had gotten for her and as he watched her, she would stop and look at her apron for a second seemingly making sure it was still clean before she moved on to the next thing she had to do. He continued to watch for a moment as she continued to cook, and he saw her spill something on the apron.

"Ahh, that's no good," said Skye, stopping what she was doing to clean her apron.

"Aprons are supposed to get dirty, right," Clyde asked, startling Skye.

"O...oh well, since you went through the trouble to get it, I'd like to keep it nice," she said as she continued to clean it.

"You seem to have plenty more to do. Where can I help," he said as he rolled up his sleeves.

"Nonsense, you just sit down. It won't take too long to finish up," Skye said, directing her full attention to Clyde.

"Really, I can help. I've worked in a kitchen before," insisted Clyde

"F...fine. Can you mince those herbs I've laid out there," Skye asked, giving in. Clyde couldn't tell if his offer to help made her happy; even though her face didn't show it, her tail certainly did as it happily swayed to and fro as she turned to continue with dinner.

The rest of the night was quite pleasant as Clyde explained what happened on his journey as well as what things he needed to do next. Followed by a half-hearted lecture from Skye before she tuckered herself out for the night.

Clyde still felt a bit undeserving as he lay in his bed thinking about all this. Oddly enough, he seemed to feel content in learning more about this new world and adjusting to his new life.

******

Clyde spent the next few days making adjustments to his armor in between helping Skaald with some various jobs. Once he had finished his armor, Skye asked him to come along with her to the market.

"So, what all are you getting," asked Clyde, wondering what she needed him for.

"Well, just the things we need for the month. It's a lot of trouble for me to carry it all myself," said Skye as she glanced down at Clyde beside her.

"Don't you go to town every other day or so? You leave the house quite often."

"Oh no, I don't go into town until we need supplies or I have a delivery to make. I go to the outskirts of town to gather herbs."

"Herbs?... For cooking," asked Clyde as he struggled to push the cart up the poorly kept road.

"Well, there are quite a few around here that are useful for cooking; although in my opinion, there's more money and usefulness from the medicinal herbs that come from this area," explained Skye as she helped push the wagon up the steep muddy road.

"That could be quite useful to know... Would you mind if I came along with you next time you go," asked Clyde as they finally made it to the well-made road.

"Yes, of course! I'd be more than happy to show you what I know!... You aren't just sweetening me up to do another foolish journey of yours, are you?"

Skye went from as excited as a puppy to as cautious as a wolf in an instant and Clyde couldn't tell if she was joking or not, so he simply answered honestly with a shake of his head.

"Wonderful! We'll set out in the morning," said Skye, back to being cheerful and excited.

They continued to the market where seemingly everyone knew and adored Skye as she seamlessly went from one store or stall to the next bringing a sack or box of something and packing it into the cart Clyde was pulling as he tried to keep up with his bright blue leader. She seemed to know almost everyone by name and Clyde could overhear her talking to everyone she went to about him for some reason. If they were close to the cart, she would bring them over and introduce them to Clyde while at the same time talking the poor store owners into giving her a discount on whatever she was purchasing. She was as smart as she was social and was using tactics that Clyde could never get away with. Following Skye around the market was far different than when Skaald brought Clyde through to introduce him around. Skaald was social and everything, but he brought a completely different atmosphere than Skye did. By the time they had finished shopping, the closing bell of the market had already struck, and it was beginning to turn dark. Clyde was exhausted from watching Skye all day, let alone the increasingly heavier cart he was pulling trying to keep up with her.

"Well, that went far better than if I would have gone alone," said Skye as she hummed walking along in front of Clyde.

"It's a miracle you can get all of this done alone," said Clyde in a strained voice as he tugged the cart along.

"Oh, usually Skaald comes along. I just wanted to introduce you to all of my friends," said Skye as she giggled mischievously.

The next morning, Clyde prepared to set out with Skye. She told Clyde to only pack his waterskin as well as a journal so he could take notes of different herbs. Once Skye was prepared, they set out. Surprisingly to Clyde, they were going toward No Man's Land which seemed somewhat alarming as he didn't bring his weapons.

"We're not going into No Man's Land are we," asked Clyde as he continued to follow Skye.

"Well, yes, just not far enough to see anything dangerous, I assure you," she said confidently.

Clyde decided to just believe her as he obediently followed her. He offered to carry the large basket that she intended to gather herbs in even though she insisted that Clyde just worry about taking notes as they went along.

After a few hours of walking, Skye finally stopped and turned to Clyde.

"Well, this is my first little patch of herbs. Are you ready to learn," she asked as she set some of her things down.

"Of course, ready when you are," Clyde said as he fumbled for his journal and sharp piece of charcoal.

They spent the first half of the day going through Skye's first patch of herbs. Clyde diligently took notes on what it looked like as well as the different uses for each one she showed him as well as how to prepare it. It wasn't exactly straight forward as Clyde had hoped because Skye took this opportunity to not only teach him about herbs but quiz Clyde on the new languages he was learning. She would suddenly start speaking Dwarvish, Elvish, or the language of her people known as Dracish. Even though Clyde had originally only asked to learn Common and Dwarvish, Skye had insisted that he learn the rest of what she knew since he was picking it up fairly quickly. Clyde could successfully hold a conversation in Dwarvish and

Elvish, but when it came to Dracish, he was having trouble. He could understand it fine and even do simple phrases but anything beyond simple, Clyde's mouth just couldn't seem to make the correct sounds as it was very difficult for him to pronounce anything. Clyde could only guess that Lizardians had a far stronger vocal range than humans. But luckily, Skye was satisfied with Clyde being able to understand it well enough. As far as writing and reading, Clyde was able to do common and Dwarvish rather easily due to them both being simple and straightforward. Unfortunately, the same couldn't be said for Elvish as it seemed to be much more precise and complex. Luckily for Clyde, Dracish didn't have a written language and was only spoken by older Lizardians, the two surviving clans and Dragons. Skye would switch between languages and make sure Clyde was understanding the information correctly as he painstakingly deciphered and answered Skye's questions as he wrote in his journal.

Once it was around midday and they had made their way to the second patch of various herbs,

Skye stopped and set the basket down she would let Clyde carry.

"Well, I'd say all of that learning worked up an appetite. Let's take us a well-deserved lunch break," Skye announced as she spread out a thin colorful blanket that was neatly packed in the basket.

"Oh wow, you made us a picnic," said Clyde, quite excited for Skye's cooking.

"Of course. We can't go all day without eating," Skye said with a bright expression on her face as she took out what she had packed.

She had half of a loaf of bread she had left over from last night's dinner which she sliced a few pieces off of before adding one of the herbs that they had gathered earlier in the morning. It looked to be some type of mushroom that was a dull orange in color. Skye said that it tastes quite good with meat or bread but by itself, it has a very strong flavor. She said that as far as usefulness, you could grind it into a paste and add a bit of salt to it and it is very good to put on small wounds. It may burn a bit but it would help kick start the healing process almost twice as fast as letting it heal naturally. It's surprisingly quite common in this area and grows where normal mushrooms would.

After Skye added the dried salted meat she must have had stored away, she gave Clyde his share.

"If it's not too much trouble since we're taking a break and all, could you tell me more about your people," asked Clyde, while examining the erotic mushroom before committing to a bite.

"Mmm?... I don't see how that could be any trouble.... Let's see... where to begin," said Skye in-between bites of her share of the lunch.

Clyde finally gave in and took a bite of his after seeing Skye enjoying it so much. It was definitely a strong flavor that could only be described as powerful. The salty taste of the meat and fresh fluffy wheat bread was followed by a powerful tangy spicy flavor with an almost milky texture as soon as the mushroom hit the tongue. It was extremely unique, but Skye was right. It was quite good all together and Clyde could easily continue to eat his share of the little lunch she prepared as she began her story.

"My people came from the dragons," is what my mother always told me. "I couldn't ever get a straight answer from any of the elders if that meant we were children of the dragons or if they created us with some magical power. They all seemed to have their own theories and answers to tell me the dragons in question were powerful creatures and strong leaders. There were five clans in total on this continent, each with their respective dragon. First, you had the fire dragon clan led by Ragon, the first flame. They settled right around this area, as a matter of fact. They were the first to declare war against the Humans who were trying to settle here and also the first to fall as the Humans slayed Ragon and the clan dispersed. Next you have the frozen tundra clan led by Crono, the iron willed, far to the north who helped Ragon fight the Humans at first but quickly took the remainder of his people far into the tundra as soon as Ragon fell. Next is my clan, the roaming wanderers led by Zaiross, the untethered. A few of our warriors joined and helped in the war. They all met the same defeat and soon after, Zaiross went into hiding; then our people slowly began to wander about integrating ourselves into the new world populated by Humans. Before the Humans came and did all of that, the Elves came from the south and wiped out the entire earth dragon clan and imprisoned their leader Irook, the unmoving. I suppose he's still alive but it's hard to tell what the Elves have done to him. Most of the southern clan either fled or are now slaves to the elves at this point. Then, finally, you have the great forest swamp clan led by the vicious poison dragon, Eridos. They didn't help any other clan, nor did they get successfully attacked due to the rough location in which they live. I've visited the clan once in my life before my clan dispersed and we wandered between the clans. They were nothing but thieves and scum, it seemed. Fortunately, the higher ups in the clan treated us nicely while we stayed there. If you ever have to go there, be extremely cautious of everyone if they even allow Humans into their swamp…. Hmm, I suppose that's all the important history I can share with you about my people.

There are apparently more clans on other continents from what the elders used to tell us. Although outside of their stories, I don't know anything about them." After she finished, she took a large drink out of her waterskin before starting to clean up the picnic.

"Interesting. It seems like your people have been through a lot... Do you resent the Humans any for what they did," asked Clyde as he helped her pack up.

"No, of course not. It was Ragon who started the war simply because he thought the Humans were pests. The only ones I would justify as in the wrong would be the Elves because they never even warned the southern clan before massacring them. Fortunately, the Elves I've met have been mostly respectful; but from what I hear, the closer you get to the Elven kingdom, the more they look down on other races. I hear that the Elven royalty and nobility are extremely hateful toward anyone that isn't an Elf."

"Hmm, there's still a lot that I don't know... Wait, if you're apparently part dragon, can you use some kind of dragon magic," Clyde asked as he remembered the recent fight he had.

"Well, I'm not sure it's what you'd expect. Our magical potential varies just like Humans. The only difference is that our aptitude is the same as our dragon leaders so that makes me proficient in both water and lighting magic; my potential is only a level two," said Skye as she showed off some sparks from her hands.

"I don't suppose you could explain what all of that means, could you," asked Clyde as his interest increased.

"Unfortunately, I don't know too much about it since I was a low level two, my options in magic were fairly limited. So other than the basics, I don't know much... Come to think of it, if you're curious about it, Skaald can introduce you to the town mage. He does some work for him from time to time," Skye said, seemingly hoping that she didn't disappoint Clyde.

"I'd definitely like to see if I can try my hand at it... but today I'll try to learn more about these interesting plants. Who knows? Maybe I'll find you some rare stuff exploring No Man's Land," said Clyde, trying to get Skye back in a cheerful mood.

It worked because Skye lit up as she beckoned Clyde on to the next patch. They spent the rest of the day going from patch to patch as Skye continued to explain different herbs and preparation details while at the same time continuing to test Clyde's language knowledge. They didn't make it back home till almost two hours past dark with the only light Clyde could follow was Skye's spell light. She made an electrical arc between her fingers making a bright blue light that illuminated about three feet around her. It was quite handy and made Clyde want to learn magic even more. Once they got home, Skye had to feed the starving Dwarf that was unusually noticeably nervous, obviously because Skye was so late getting home. Clyde could tell that they really cared for one another. After they settled in and ate, Clyde prepared for the next day where he would meet this town mage and see if he could learn any magic.

The following day, Clyde spent the better half of the day continuing to help Skye with her herbalist orders as she showed him the proper methods to prepare and change the effects of select herbs and what mixtures did what. By the time Skaald returned from his morning errands and was ready to take Clyde to meet the mage, Clyde had gotten fairly good at what Skye was showing him. Although Skye seemed disappointed that her pupil was being taken away, she didn't offer any way as to stop Clyde from going and she continued her work on her own.

"So, can you tell me anything about this mage," Clyde asked as Skaald and he ventured down the muddy path.

"Well, he's quite full of himself but as far as being an actual mage, he hasn't done anything to outright help the town in any way so other than the few jobs he has me do, I don't know anything about him."

This was an unusual response from Skaald, as the rest of the people he had introduced to Clyde, he always had something positive to say about them. So, Clyde instantly got the impression that this guy may not exactly be a teacher like Clyde had hoped.

Soon enough they had come to their destination. It was a large two-story building with boarded up windows and a very run-down exterior. Skaald reluctantly knocked on the door and awaited a response. After a short while of waiting, the door suddenly made a "click" and opened just slightly. After a moment, it finally swung open revealing a scrawny man with long unkempt hair and a tangled mess of a beard.

"Who's the poor excuse of a bodyguard behind you, blacksmith?... Never mind, come quickly," said the man as he quickly disappeared back into the house.

Skaald waited a moment supposedly for the man to get outside of earshot and turned to Clyde almost whispering,

"Good luck, you poor excuse of a bodyguard." He said this laughing to himself as he saw Clyde's irritated expression.

They quickly entered following the man back into the house. Surprisingly, Clyde noticed that the inside was quite tidy giving almost the complete opposite impression that the outside of the house gave. There were more books than Clyde could count organized on many different shelves throughout the house as well as many small plants that are somehow doing well given the lack of sunlight. It was rather dark with the house only being illuminated by a candle here and there, but it was still light enough to see just how neat the house was kept. When they finally arrived at the room where Skaald apparently had to do work, he dropped his tools and began working away without as much as a question to the mage. Clyde decided this was his opportunity to ask whatever he could, so he turned to the mage who, surprisingly, was staring uncomfortably at Clyde giving Clyde a startle as he looked into the wide-eyed gaze of the mage.

"You want something…. Go ahead. Let's hear it then," said the mage as soon as he noticed Clyde glancing back at him.

"Uh… I'm wanting to learn more about magic. I was told you could tell me what I need to know," said Clyde after he quickly gathered himself.

"Well, I suppose I can't get anything else done until he's finished. Follow me." The mage didn't waste any time as he quickly went into the next room.

Clyde followed behind him. As he walked in, the mage waved his hand. As many candles that were scattered around instantly lit up brightening the room as if you would flip a switch. He then sat down in an old large chair and motioned for Clyde to do the same.

"What is it you'd like to know… How to imbue your sword in flame or how to topple your enemies with a flick of your finger…. All of you young tough wanna be knights are the same so which dream do you want me to crush first," said the old man in a very crude tone as he began flipping through a book he had lying beside him.

"Well, I don't need anything like that, although it wouldn't hurt to know about it honestly. I don't know the first thing about magic other than it exists," said Clyde, trying to ignore the mage's tone.

The mage seemed taken aback by Clyde's question as he paused for a moment simply glancing up from his book staring at Clyde.

"Tsk, you're telling me that you, a grown man, don't know anything about magic. Have you been living under a rock or are you just dense in the head," asked the mage in an increasingly irritated tone.

"Why don't we go with the former option to keep things rolling. I assume you don't want to talk to someone that has trouble understanding you," said Clyde, gaining some confidence to fight back in this conversation.

"Fine, we'll start at the beginning. But don't expect me to slow down and repeat myself," said the mage as he slapped his book shut.

"I'd hate to make a man of your stature have to belittle himself into repeating what his wise words said for such a dense bodyguard such as myself. Please continue," said Clyde, expressing his own irritation.

"Hmm, you're clever but a stupid clever. You'd best pay attention. First, you have your magical potential gauged on a scale of one to five. If you're a level one, you can only do basic magic and will never amount to much as a mage. If you're at a high enough level, you can potentially use any magic you wish. It just might be more difficult to learn. Along with your level, you have aptitudes that decide what kind of magic you'll be good at. If you're at a high enough level, however, you can potentially use any magic you wish. For example, you have your basic elemental aptitudes: fire, wind, water, and earth as well as some rare aptitudes such as dark, light, enhancement, and healing. There are many more rare aptitudes but the test you take is only able to show those."

"There's a test you can take," asked Clyde, interrupting the mage.

"... Yes, I'll get to that, so shut it, and listen. Ahem! You can have more than one aptitude. In fact, it's rare to only have one. Usually, most people have two. As for myself, I'm a level three mage with aptitudes in fire and telekinesis magic. I'm also proficient in water and wind magic through years of practice. The only drawback to using other magic is it takes more mana or energy to use."

The mage stopped for a second and began rustling through some papers he had on a table beside him.

"Since I'm a kingdom anointed town mage, it is my duty to allow everyone to test their magical abilities. So, since you're here and I'm bored, let's try it," said the mage as he produced a paper with strange writing surrounding a handprint.

"Simply place your hand on the handprint and this paper will tell me all about you."

Clyde obeyed the mage and placed his hand on the paper; however, nothing seemed to happen. After a moment, the mage made a confused "huh" before taking the paper away from Clyde and placing his hand on it. Instantly, the paper began to glow and certain words on the paper lit up brightly.

"Well, that's what's supposed to happen here. Try it with this one," said the mage as he produced another paper.

Nothing happened yet again as Clyde laid his hand on the paper, making the mage even more frustrated.

"Surely you're not that low of a level. This even shows a level one bright as day and no one is lower than that." The mage quickly began flipping through books here and there through the room as Clyde sat there just as confused.

"Well, it seems to me that you have absolutely no magical potential, so you're quite useless here," said the mage bluntly.

"Well, would there be any way that I could still borrow some of your books so I can learn more about it? Regardless, if I can use it or not, it's still handy to know since it's everywhere around me," said Clyde as he folded the paper into his pocket while the mage wasn't looking.

"Hmm... I don't feel comfortable letting you borrow them... but you're welcome to stop by and read them so long as you bring me something to eat in return," said the mage as Skaald poked his head in the room.

"Everything is fixed. Are you ready to go Clyde," asked Skaald, seemingly in a hurry to leave.

"If you are," replied Clyde

After they left the mage's house, they quietly walked back home. Right before they turned down the street, Skaald spoke up.

"I wouldn't worry about not being able to use magic. It's more of a burden than anything, I swear," he said clearly, attempting to cheer Clyde up.

"Thanks, but I'm not that worried about it. I had assumed that I wouldn't be able to use it but luckily, he's going to let me use his library to learn about it," explained Clyde.

"Don't get me wrong but what's the point in learning about it if you can't use it, boy?"

"Well, the more I know about it, the less of a problem it will be if I fight someone or something that uses it," said Clyde, remembering his fight in the northern town.

"I see... Well, if I were you, I'd definitely avoid fighting anyone stronger than level three. Because once you're fighting something or someone that strong, death isn't far behind," warned Skaald before they finally made it back home.

Once they went inside and told Skye the news, she also, like Skaald, assumed Clyde was sad and tried cheering him up by coddling him. Although Clyde tried to get away from her, he was ultimately overpowered by Skye as she hugged him, petting his head. After she finally released him, they had a nice dinner and went off to bed, making an end to the long day.

Clyde spent the next few weeks learning all he could from the mage's library of books as well as from Skye as she continued to take Clyde out to learn about herbs and work on his language skills. Clyde was definitely glad to learn the different languages as the various books the mage had were indeed written in different ones. The mage was absolutely surprised that Clyde could read any book that he had and eventually started opening up and even expecting Clyde to visit once he got his chores done with Skye.

"Hey mage, can you explain what this other magic is," asked Clyde after finding a magic that originated from nature instead of oneself.

"Mmm, it's about time you started using my name. I'm sick of you calling me mage. The name's Oliver," he said as he finished eating the dinner Skye had made for Clyde to bring him.

Clyde assumed she would be more willing to make it if he said it was for himself since she decided she didn't like him after Clyde and Skaald got home that day. The types of magic Clyde had learned about were nothing very important, just the basics of how a mage should get started in the four basic elements as well as different diagrams showing the supposed best stance to conjure your magic. This one seemed to apparently be a completely different type of magic that used natural mana instead of your own which Clyde was optimistic to see if he could learn such a magic.

"Ahh, that's the olden magic," said Oliver as he leaned over Clyde's shoulder.

"Unfortunately, you still would be unable to use it but it is very different from the common magic that most people use today. The magic that's most commonly used comes from the person's own mana, so depending on your level is how powerful a magic you're able to use. Now, for the olden magic, you use a small amount of your personal mana to control a vast amount of natural mana to perform your desired spell. It is technically the most powerful form of magic, but you have to know exactly what you're doing in order to perform it correctly. It takes a ridiculous amount of knowledge about elements and nature as well as mana control to perform so most people don't even consider using it," he explained as he pulled a few more books from some shelves.

"Here are a few examples of some talented wizards using this magic. The first is when the Humans first came to this continent and the great mage of the Humans used an earth-shaking lightning blast to bring down the fire dragon. The second was a grand earthquake that opened up the mountain for the Dwarves to make their home in," explained Oliver as he showed Clyde the storybooks.

"I see... Are there any famous wizards these days that use this type of magic," asked Clyde.

"There's two that I know of... One is a talented level five mage belonging to some guild close to the capital and the second is a level four that teaches in the mage school close to the Elven kingdom. Oddly enough, neither of them has accomplished anything as miraculous as these two yet but, then again, I wouldn't go testing their abilities anytime soon," he said as he sat back down in his favorite chair.

Clyde soon realized that Oliver wasn't as bad of a person as he let on even though he definitely didn't like people and preferred to be alone studying his many books and practicing his magic. Apparently, he graduated from the college he mentioned and was anointed by the king to serve as a royal mage. Although he isn't a high-ranking royal mage, it's still an impressive accomplishment from what Clyde read about in the various books. Apparently, if you choose to be classified as a mage, you're tested and ranked by either the college, the guild board, or the king. The most accurate is the college from what I understand but the most meaningful, if you want to do something with your magic, is through the king or the guild board. The reason I've heard is they're not as accurate is that they only measure your magical combat ability instead of your magic as a whole. Every large town in the king's territory has an appointed mage to either find strong potential mages or to help protect the town from any potential threats. Clyde couldn't help but wonder if Oliver could even look at a Gex let alone fight one.

After Clyde was satisfied with learning about the different aspects of magic, for the time being he began to set his sights back to his goals and began preparing to hunt and kill a Gex.

Clyde spent the next week preparing for his next goal. Skaald helped him quite a lot, tweaking his armor and honing his sword and kukri. He also helped Clyde design a new weapon specifically for fighting a Gex. After some thought and recommendations from Skaald, Clyde settled on making a short sword spear type of weapon using the arm of the Gex he brought in. The blade was cut at about two and a half feet and was securely attached to a high-quality treated handle he got Darren to order for him. The end was fixed with a small but heavy counterweight giving the weapon a unique balance that was comfortable to wield either one or two handed. The length altogether was five feet so it would be easily packable for Clyde to carry without worry.

"Well, not sure if it'll kill a Gex but it might come in handy for something whenever you head out again," said Skaald as he was flipping the weapon around.

"Well, hopefully it'll do whatever I need it to... I suppose I'll be ready to head out by next week if Darren gets the supplies I ordered in."

"What plans have you got until then," asked Skaald as he set the weapon down.

"Nothing in particular. I think Darren needed some help whenever his shipment came in so I'm free until then. "What did you have in mind", asked Clyde, curious as to what Skaald's intentions were.

"Well, Skye is wanting to make a round through town tomorrow to deliver the rest of her orders.

I've got word that a caravan was coming into town tomorrow as well. Maybe you could accompany her just to give me a little piece of mind," he said as he scratched his head poking at the fire in the forge.

Caravans are not uncommon in this town. Different ones come from time to time varying in size and usually bringing a lot of different people along, both good and bad. Clyde assumed that's why he wanted him to go, to just make sure Skye doesn't end up getting robbed or worse.

"Yea, I don't mind tagging along with her. I'd like to shop around the caravan myself anyway," said Clyde, trying to assure Skaald.

Clyde also assumed it was going to be a busy day for Skaald to man his stall as the adventurers and guards that follow the caravan will buy new weapons and armor as well as repair their current equipment.

Clyde then left Skaald to find Skye to let her know he wants to go with her tomorrow. He found her in the kitchen at her little worktable where she prepared herbs. She was grinding away with her mortar and pestle in her own little world.

"Skye... I hear you're going into town tomorrow," said Clyde, getting her attention.

"Huh?... Oh yes, I've got to deliver these orders... It seems I get more and more every month," she said as she looked over at the wagon she had borrowed from Darren that was filled with neatly wrapped concoction for various uses that Skye had prepared.

"Would you mind if I tagged along with you tomorrow to help deliver them all?"

"Oh never... but you don't have to. I'm sure you've got things you'd rather be doing," she said as she seemed to not want to burden Clyde. She turned away from him to hide her face even though her tail swished with excitement to hear Clyde's response.

Clyde thought about teasing her and seeing how she would react, but he also didn't want to make her angry. After a moment of thought, he decided on his answer.

"Well, I couldn't stand to let you pull that heavy wagon all the way to town. What kind of a friend would... besides, I'll need the wagon to carry what I plan to buy so I guess I not only want to, but I have to go with you," argued Clyde, trying to hide his light teasing.

Sykes' tail stopped for a moment making Clyde a bit nervous but then she turned around with a bright smile on her face.

"Of course, then, you have to go with me tomorrow. There's no way around it! I'll pack us a lunch," she said as she came over to Clyde giving him a light hug before she went on over to grab her lunch basket to have it ready for tomorrow. After she packed the lunch, Clyde decided to spend the rest of the day helping her finish up her herbalist orders and packing them all up neatly and securely on the cart.

The next morning, Clyde was getting ready to go double checking the cart and things. Although he usually wears his armor and brings his weapons and helmet, he decided it would be more trouble than it was worth carrying them attached to his waist so he ultimately trying to pull the cart with his weapons and helmet on his waist, so he ultimately decided to leave them behind. Skye called as she was ready to leave while Clyde was attempting to unlatch his helmet from his belt, and he hurried along to join her.

"If we hurry, we can get ahead of the crowd before the market bell tolls," said Skye helping Clyde push the wagon along the deeply mudded road until they made it to the paved part of town.

She was quite aware of the caravan coming to town and was quite right to hurry along because, from what Clyde understood, whenever a caravan came through, the town got insanely busy with people going to and fro buying and selling to the traveling caravan. Sadly, despite their effort to hurry once they got to the main street, there was already many people, horses, and buggies making their way to a spot to set up or prepare for the morning bell to go off to make a profit. Skye and Clyde decided it would be best to take the backstreets to the few houses she made personal deliveries to. Clyde obediently followed her lead as she navigated in between houses and buildings, stopping at various places. She took their order inside as Clyde stayed out with the cart, and almost every house they went to Clyde could hear Skye strike up a conversation with her clients. She would ask about whatever they needed the herbs for, if they were working well, if there's any new changes, and so on almost like a caring doctor would. Then she would have a lengthy conversation about the weather or how things have been and all of that. Clyde couldn't help but enjoy hearing each person's different reaction to Skye as she talked and seemed to make some of the older folks' day better. Finally, after the last personal house visit, they made their way to the town doctor's place. They hadn't even distributed a fourth of the prepared medicines and concoctions, so Clyde was curious as to just how much they were going to deliver here. It was long past the morning market bell time and beginning to be close to midday.

They took the cart around the front of the building to the loading dock, and it was immediately evident that the town was completely filled with people both from the caravan and town alike with barely enough room for anyone else. Clyde forced his way into the chaos and successfully over to the loading dock without much issue. Skye went in to tell the town doctor that they were here, and to ask where he wanted everything and as Clyde waited at the cart to hear something, Dr. Montgomery came out.

"Well, I didn't take you for a delivery boy," said Montgomery, teasing Clyde.

"Better than a stock boy... Are you working here now," asked Clyde as he jabbed back.

"Yea, I figured I'd best put myself to some use since you were kind enough to throw me back into being a doctor."

"That's far better than being beaten sober in a dark alley... Where do you want these," Clyde asked as he handed Montgomery an armful of the packages.

"F... follow me...," he said as he was struggling with the load he was carrying.

Clyde and Montgomery piled them in the correct area and Clyde noticed there were some still in the cart.

"Have you gotten all you're supposed to get?"

"Yup, we ordered fifty varying concoctions and from my list we've got them all.... You had better get Mrs. Everflair and head on out," said Montgomery as he noticed some out-of-town customers beginning to enter the store.

"How come? She's not causing any trouble is she," asked Clyde, assuming she's talking the other doctor to death.

"You seriously don't know? I'll make it quick. People outside of this town normally openly hate Lizardians... so much so that they may cause some trouble." He quickly explained pushing Clyde into the back door of the Doctors office.

Clyde made his way to the front where Skye and the doctor had been talking and Clyde instantly got angry upon seeing Skye. He looked across the room and saw her sitting in a chair beside the doctor surrounded by four people. Her dress was soaking wet from what seemed to be the contents of a bucket one of the people was holding. Tears were rolling down her face even though she didn't make a sound indicating she was crying.

"Well, dang sorry, doc. I couldn't clean this filth out of your store. Looks like we're gonna have to try a bit harder gang," said what seemed to be the ringleader.

As Clyde approached them, he instinctively sized them up. They seemed like adventurers with a reasonable amount of experience. There were three men: two with swords on their sides and one with a large axe. The last was a woman that seemed small but confident. Clyde assumed she was a mage due to the staff she carried which was normally used to help control one's magic more carefully.

"Huh? Oh, look at those eyes (ha ha). You must be one of those lizard lovers I hear..."

"I'll only ask once... Apologize to my friend and there won't be any problems," said Clyde cutting him off. Clyde was already expecting a dumb response, so he unlatched his helmet from his waist and gripped it tightly as he waited for an answer.

"Ha, what a loo..." (wham!!)

Clyde uppercut him with his helmet causing him to almost bite his tongue completely off. As blood flew through the air as the first man was falling to the ground, Clyde wasted no time as he reared back his leg. (Wham!!) Another powerful hit this time. Clyde gave everything he had into kicking the large man with the axe square in the nethers, dropping him to his knees in unimaginable pain. Clyde had lost his element of surprise as he caught in the corner of his eye the mage girl preparing some spell. As quick as a reflex before she could cast the spell (klunk!!) Clyde had nailed her in the head with his helmet, giving him a few moments to deal with the last one who had drawn his sword and was fully prepared for Clyde's to make his next move.

"You think you can take out my comrades like that and leave here unscathed? Who do you think you are," asked the man as he prepared to attack Clyde.

Clyde prepared to use his vambraces to deflect the sword and either disarm him or get a few solid hits in. Just as the man raised his sword to attack Clyde, (boom) a flash of blue hit the man laying him out cold on the floor. It was a very powerful fist from a very upset Skye. Clyde didn't have time to console her as he noticed the mage was recovering from her hit. Clyde walked over and confronted her with a cold unforgiving stare.

"I...I yield. We're so sorry. We won't do it again," said the girl caving from Clyde's intense pressure.

"It's too late for apologies. Get your scum friends out of here before I quit being generous." Clyde turned his back to the frightened girl and walked over to Skye.

He took her arm and quietly led her out of the office back to the cart. He was then jerked around and slapped by a still crying Skye.

"Why did you do that! You should have just let them have their fun and they would have left. You shouldn't put yourself in dang..." Skye was cut off by Clyde hugging her tightly.

"You've done far too much for me to have me stand by and watch people treat you like that. I don't care how angry you get with me as long as I can, I will stop that from happening to you," said Clyde, letting her go and picking up the cart.

"We've still got some deliveries to make... but let me stop by Darren's first," said Clyde, leading the way to Darren's. Skye, at a loss for words, simply followed obediently.

Once Skye and Clyde made it to Darren's store and went into the back door like Clyde usually did, they met Darren coming out of his stockroom.

"My gosh! What happened to you, Mrs. Skye? Is everything alright," asked Darren as he sat down what he was carrying and rushed over to check on her.

"I'm f... fine, really, don't worry yourself," Skye said, reassuring Darren who, like Clyde, cared a great deal for Skye.

"You wouldn't happen to have some spare clothes in the back for her would you Darren," asked Clyde as he pulled a chair up for Skye to sit in, which she did.

"Of course, give me just a moment," he said as he rushed back into his storeroom.

"Hey, you rest here for a bit, alright Skye? I'm going to go finish delivering the herbs."

"No, I'm fine. You don't have to... ah," she tried to say as she was standing to her feet. Clyde grabbed her by the shoulders before she was all the way up and forced her back down in the chair.

"I know you're fine, but we don't have that many left to deliver. I'll make up for our lost time going alone... I can remember where they're supposed to go from when we took the orders. You better take this chance to rest because when I get back, we're going to go shopping together at the caravan. Maybe they have some exotic food to try or some good books to buy," Clyde said as Skye looked up at him after being sat down. She was met with the best fake smile Clyde could muster. He wasn't faking to lie to her, but rather comfort her enough to listen.

"Fine... I do plan on staying until the market closes since I'll be well rested and all," said Skye quite seriously as she gently pushed Clyde toward the door.

"Also, you'd best be nice and ask how everyone is doing for me. I expect a detailed response of everyone you have left to deliver to," she added, looking away from Clyde almost as if she was pouting.

"Here, this should fit you nicely," Darren said as he handed Skye a box of dry clothes.

Darren followed Clyde out of the room so Skye could change clothes.

"So, what exactly happened? She's not hurt or anything is she," asked Darren quietly as he followed Clyde.

"No, I don't think they hurt her physically but what they did was almost unspeakable," said Clyde holding back his frustration of the subject.

"Usually when a caravan comes along, there are people that talk poorly about seeing her. Usually, Skaald is with her to prevent anything from happening to her... She could most definitely defend herself as you well know but she's far too kind to hurt anyone," said Darren as they stopped by the door.

"If I knew it was going to be this bad, I wouldn't have left her side for a second... Hey, could I borrow that," asked Clyde as he pointed to a small sword laying on the table.

"Surely you aren't going to cause any trouble, are you? I mean, yes, you can borrow it but it's not worth killing them."

"It's nothing like that, I just have a feeling that they might come back... I didn't exactly finish the job so they may have some friends come after me. I'd rather be prepared," said Clyde, strapping the sword to his waist.

"I'd hate to know what you did to them. Try to avoid getting yourself hurt. You know Skye would never forgive me if you did."

"Hopefully I can avoid any contact at all until I get back," said Clyde, lifting the wagon and preparing to head on.

"I'll take good care of Skye, don't worry," said Darren as Clyde was still within earshot.

Clyde went to the next couple of houses without much trouble. He was as nice as he could be asking the questions he heard Skye ask earlier that morning. All the people asked about Skye, worried that she was sick or injured, then told Clyde some story of how they knew Skye for so long and what all she does for them. Clyde understood how the townspeople all think so highly of her because she's been in the town for fifty or so years building a positive strong relationship with all of them. Clyde didn't have the heart to tell any of them what happened because he blamed himself for letting it happen in the first place. He only told them she wasn't feeling too well so he was delivering for her. Everything was going well and Clyde only had two more stops to make before he could go back and make good on his promise. At this point, he was feeling terribly guilty that Skye went through something so terrible, and he was hoping that she would forgive him after they enjoyed the rest of the evening. Clyde was lost in his own thoughts as he turned the corner of one of the backstreets to head to his next stop. But something stopped him.

Clyde looked down the street and saw three people walking toward him with their weapons drawn. He then glanced behind him only to see two more with a very similar look about them. *Looks like my promise is going to be harder to keep than I thought,* he thought to himself as he pulled the cart to the side of the street and set it down before confronting the coming trouble.

"So, this is the ballsy lizard lover you were talking about? He doesn't look like much. How did he take down all three of them himself," said one beside the girl Clyde left mostly unharmed.

"Hey! I heard you ruffled up some of my friends earlier. Have you got anything you'd like to say before we get down to business," he said as he confidently stepped closer to Clyde.

Clyde gave them all a quick look before he answered. They were all carrying blunt sticks in their hands with swords and such on their waists, so Clyde assumed they weren't going to outright kill him. This gave Clyde a few options to consider. Firstly, he could decide to fight with his fists or his sword. If he chose poorly, it most definitely would have a poor ending. Even attempting to fight back fairly, the odds were not in Clyde's favor. The only option he could think of was to try and talk them down to at least not killing him, so he prepared to do so.

"They were quite rude to my herbalist master and was threatening to do more to her... so I gave them the opportunity to leave peacefully but ended up having to defend myself. I apologize if I caused you unnecessary trouble," Clyde said as he raised his hands showing he surrendered.

"Is that how it went down, Pix," asked the man as he looked back at the girl who seemed to be extremely uncomfortable.

"Y...yes," she said quietly. The man looked back at Clyde.

"I respect that you were so up front about it, but I don't think my boys and I can just let a lizard lover like you get away unscathed... we'll have to teach you your place. After all, can't have you doing something else stupid," said the man as he walked closer to Clyde.

"I have a proposal for you," said Clyde, somewhat shocking the man then making him laugh.

"Ha, ha, what could you possibly offer me right now. I hope you understand what kind of situation you're in," said the man waiting to hear what Clyde had to say.

"If I sit here and take this willingly, I want you to be respectful later when I take the Lizardian shopping through the caravan," said Clyde so full of confidence it seemed to unnerve the man in front of him.

The man stood there and thought for a moment before he spoke.

"Alright, I'll agree to that. Any man willing to take this for another, even if it's a low down Lizardian, should at least be able to ask that much. After this, I'll tell my boys to look the other way when she's around until we leave. You have my word."

Clyde could oddly tell that the man was serious as he looked Clyde square in the eyes and spoke sincerely. Clyde nodded his head and took the sword off his waist and set it in the cart. He then kneeled down in front of the group. Clyde noticed before the first hit struck him that the girl was off to the side looking right at Clyde in shock of his actions. Once Clyde came to, he was in excruciating pain as he lay there in the mud. Even through his armor, he could tell that he was quite thoroughly beaten. He forced himself to his feet and leaned on the cart until his head quit spinning.

"Hopefully that's the last time I'll have to go through that," he said as he took some cloth he had on the cart and wiped the mud and blood from his face and hands.

By the best he could tell, he had been there for about an hour, so he still had plenty of time to finish delivering and make it back to Skye. Before he headed on his way, he noticed that the girl was standing near him leaning against the wall just watching him.

Clyde then spit a bloody spot by her feet before he forced himself to lift the cart and begin to walk. He was stopped by the girl stepping in front of him.

"Why..." she simply asked as her stunned face seemed to turn to anger. "Why would you take up for that disgusting creature," she said as she stomped over to Clyde still leaning against the cart.

"That 'disgusting creature' took me in when I had nowhere else to go and has looked after me time and time again. So, why don't you tell me who's truly the disgusting creature, the kind and thoughtful Lizardian who cares far more than anyone I've ever met or the Humans who take advantage of her kindness just to throw water on her and put her down with your words breaking her heart." Clyde then spit a bloody spot by her feet before he forced himself to lift the cart and began to walk; however, she stepped right in front of him.

"Do you have any idea what they did to our people in the war? They slaughtered thousands," she said as she punched Clyde in the face out of her apparent anger of the subject.

"Yea, I do know what history says, but guess what? I wasn't alive hundreds of years ago and neither was you. So, whatever they did in the past doesn't affect me in the slightest," said Clyde as he walked around the stubborn girl.

The girl followed Clyde for some reason as he made it to the second to last two houses he had to deliver to. Luckily, they were side by side and other than their concern for Clyde's unexpected appearance, the conversations were the same as they asked about Skye and told a story or two. Once Clyde left the houses, he noticed that the girl was still there, in even more shock that these people talked so highly of a Lizardian.

"If you keep following me, you'll have to face her again... Do you think you can after what you've heard," asked Clyde as he noticed that the girl was still following him for some reason.

"I... I want to apologize... Do you think I can," she asked with a complicated expression on her face.

"That's up to you and her... personally you'll have to do a lot more than follow me around like a sad puppy to earn my forgiveness," Clyde said honestly as he still didn't like the girl for what all she'd done.

They made it back to Darren's and after Clyde calmed Darren down after seeing the state Clyde was in, Clyde took the girl to see Skye who was waiting for Clyde to return. When they entered the room, Skye had her back to the door seemingly expecting Clyde to be back alone as she spoke loudly without looking at him.

"You're late! You should have been back hours ago... Did Mrs Evoline keep you for too long?" She referred to one of the more talkative ladies Clyde had delivered to.

"Well... something like that I suppose," said Clyde, turning away to hide his beaten face from Skye so the girl would be able to say something before Skye got riled up.

Skye turned around and seemed at a loss for words at first but then she spoke up.

"How is your head? Clyde didn't hit you too hard, did he," she said in her normal concerned tone as she beckoned the girl over.

"U...uh no, I'm fine. That's not why I came... I... wanted to apologize for me and my friends... I nev..." Skye cut her off as she practically leaped from her chair and rushed over to the girl, seemingly frightening her terribly as she backed herself against the wall. Skye checked her head thoroughly before letting the poor girl go.

"You're not fine, it's beginning to bruise! Here I have something to help it heal a bit," said Skye as she applied some medicine she had on hand.

The girl, seemingly at a complete loss for any straight thought let alone words, simply bowed to Skye then left the room without saying anything. Skye then got a good look at Clyde as her jaw dropped and tears began filling her eyes.

"What happened? What did they do to you? My gosh! I can't believe you're still standing!" Skye was getting more worked up the more blood and bruises she saw on Clyde.

Clyde stopped her and got her to sit back down in the chair after a bit of bickering.

"Listen, I fell and hurt myself pretty badly but I'm fine. That girl just so happened to help me out a bit and wanted to come apologize to you for what she did. I'm feeling fine for now so let's go enjoy the caravan while we have the chance," said Clyde, wiping Sykes' tears from her eyes. She knew Clyde was lying but she seemed like she didn't know what to say and before she could collect her thoughts, Clyde grabbed her by the arm and led her into town.

They enjoyed the rest of the evening very well as Clyde noticed a few glances from people that seemingly turned away to continue whatever they were doing. It seemed that they held up their end of the deal which Clyde found some comfort in. Skye, although concerned and helping Clyde as much as he would let her get away with, seemed to have a grand time. There were in fact some exotic foods that Clyde had never even heard of. Skye seemed quite familiar with them and made Clyde taste every weird thing she could find. Clyde had bought a few books in Elvish and Dwarvish to continue his studies and Skye proceeded to empty the rest of his wallet buying food and little trinkets that she liked. At one of the last places they went to before the market closed, Clyde bought Skye a nice dress as well as Skaald a pair of goggles so he would quit complaining about getting sparks in his eyes. Once they got home, what energy Clyde had was completely gone and the pain was beginning to really set in. Skye had to help him take his armor off and she couldn't help but to put some healing ointment on his wounds and help him to bed.

"Thanks for watching after her boy... I hate that they put you in this kind of shape though you should have run," said Skaald as he came to check on Clyde after Skye finally went to sleep leaving them alone.

"Honestly, I'd do it again tomorrow if I had to... she doesn't deserve to be treated so poorly," said Clyde as he tried to set up and talk to Skaald. He stopped Clyde from sitting up immediately after.

"If she hears you straining like that, you'll be stuck in bed for an extra week before she quits taking care of you," said Skaald, smiling with a wink.

"Guess I'd better listen to her then and rest up or she'll never let me out of this bed," Clyde said as they shared a quiet laugh before Skaald left.

It took Clyde nearly a week to recover and a full week to escape from Skye's intensive care so that he could begin working and saving money again. Skye was simply making double sure Clyde was alright, but she was quite insisting that Clyde stay on bed rest until he was fully better. After a while, Clyde got sick of staying in bed and decided to sneak out before Skye had woken up and began helping Darren in his shop. It was almost time for Clyde to go back into No Man's Land and hunt a Gex down so while he was getting back to one hundred percent, he was working gaining the money and supplies he needed.

Chapter 4: Fighting Fire Without Fire

Clyde helped Darren off and on for about two weeks or so before he decided it was time to prepare his armor and weapons for his hunt. With Skaald's experienced help, Clyde was done in no time. Before Clyde began to pack his equipment away, Skaald spoke up.

"Put it on, let's give your gear a proper test," Skaald said as he opened a chest off in the corner.

"What do you mean by test," asked Clyde as he strapped his sword to his waist.

"Well, the best way to test a new weapon out is a good old sparring match," Skaald said as he put a heavy chest plate on and secured the straps.

"You can fight," asked Clyde curiously.

"Well, back in my prime I worked in an adventurer's guild. Well, more like a mercenary guild I suppose since the only thing we did right was war. And since I go through the trouble of making all these weapons, I might as well know how to use them," explained Skaald as he pulled a longsword off the wall that Clyde assumed was a display piece.

"You sure you wanna spar using real weapons," said Clyde concerningly.

"How would you know if your weapon was up to par if you didn't test it out? It'll be fine, boy. Come on," Skaald said as he opened the door for Clyde leading to the small yard outside.

Once they were both in the yard facing one another, Skaald began stretching and cracking his old bones in preparation. Once he seemed to finish, he picked up his sword. Once he got into his stance and looked at Clyde, he could instantly tell that Skaald was no novice when It came to fighting. Clyde decided to go against his initial thought of going easy and taking Skaald seriously as he drew his short spear in preparation for the sparring match.

"We'll start when this coin hits the dirt. We've only got one good spar before the old lady gets mad at me for pushing you so hard before you're fully healed so don't hold back boy..." As soon as Skaald finished, he flipped the coin high into the air and resumed his stance.

Clyde kept his eyes locked on Skaald as he tightened his grip on his spear. Skaald's expression was cold and calculated as if he was ready for anything Clyde could throw his way. Clyde noticed the coin flash in his vision on its way to the ground. The spar had begun. Clyde decided to take the offensive and as soon as the coin hit the dirt, he made a strong overhead slash with his spear that was met with Skaald's blade. He angled his blade to throw Clyde's spear off to the side, then Clyde simply used the momentum and balance of the spear to reposition and then thrust toward Skaald again. When Clyde stepped forward to follow through with his thrust, he lost his footing as he noticed Skaald was using his off hand to apparently use some earth magic to move the earth beneath Clyde's feet. Clyde couldn't catch himself and fell to his knees. Skaald took the opportunity to close the distance and make a strike toward Clyde. Clyde used his spear handle to block the sword as he jumped to his feet drawing his kukri and making a fast slash toward Skaald. Skaald wasted no time as he shoved his palm into Clyde's chest sending him right back into the dirt. Clyde continued to roll back using the momentum to roll backwards till he hit his feet again. Although Clyde couldn't hold onto his kukri, he managed to keep hold of the spear and used it to prepare for Skaald's next move which came with almost no hesitation as he lunged forward towards Clyde. Clyde took a quick step back to use his reach as an advantage on his spear as he took a powerful side slash toward Skaald. It was easily blocked. Clyde just as easily retracted and swung a second strike which was blocked just as easily and before Clyde could manage a third, Skaald quickly used another earth spell on the ground beneath him to quickly gain ground on Clyde who was in mid swing and very defenseless. Skaald punched Clyde in the gut with all his might. It seemed as if Clyde hit the ground fast. Despite Clyde's armor, Skaald's punch was quite decisive as it took Clyde's breath away. The fight was decided. As Clyde struggled to his feet, Skaald grabbed his arm and helped him. As they walked back toward the house, Clyde noticed Skye standing in the doorway with an upset expression on her face.

"You could have refrained from using your magic; he's still injured after all," said Skye as she pecked Skaald on the head with her mortar.

"He's a sharp boy. He can handle a little rough sparring. It's good for his health," Skaald said, shielding his head from Skye's attacks.

Clyde was still unable to speak as he was trying to regain his breath. Clyde then thought to himself that even if he wasn't hurt, Skaald would have won just as easily, making Clyde feel that he is not even close to being ready to accomplish his goal.

"Listen, boy, don't beat yourself up over the loss. I've got at least a few centuries on you in fighting experience," said Skaald as he sat Clyde down in a chair.

Clyde managed to speak after a few minutes. "Will... you... help me get better at fighting Skaald,"

Clyde asked weakly as he was still getting his breath back.

"Hmmm... I can spar with you again and see if you improve any but I'm no fighting teacher. If you're okay with that, I'll do what I can," said Skaald, sitting down beside Clyde.

Clyde nodded his head in agreement, and they did just that. They sparred once every day after they finished the work for the day. Clyde learned more about how magic worked than he ever could reading books. Especially the combat aspect of it from what he had observed from Skaald mopping the floor with him every day for a week. Apparently once you have the hang of certain spells, the time it takes to cast them reduces drastically from how long it says it takes to cast them in the various books. Although the results may be weaker, the speed is the greater advantage in a real fight. Skaald said he hardly even thinks of what spell he's about to use while he's fighting which makes it more difficult for Clyde to understand how it works. Fortunately, he had noticed one thing that helps during their daily fights. When Skaald activates a spell, the motion of his hand shows which direction the spell will most likely come from and although that wouldn't help with every magic user Clyde would ever fight, he was certain that it was a great thing to look for in his future encounters. On the fifth day of their routine, Clyde decided to give it his all again now that his spear was tweaked to its most ideal balance, and he had learned enough that he had no excuse to lose.

"I have a few questions before we start," asked Clyde as he tightened his armor in preparation.

"Go ahead and ask, boy," said Skaald as he was getting used to a different weapon like he had every day. Today he had a long Warhammer.

"Where did you learn to fight so well," Clyde asked, hoping for some grand story.

"Oh, I guess I should have told you... I used to be a blacksmith for a mercenary guild about a century ago. There were a few small wars going on so for a merc guild, if you couldn't fight you wasn't going to live very long. Since I made so many different weapons, I figured I'd learn how to use anything I ever made through spars like this with my guild mates. I eventually got to a point where there were only a few that could beat me back in the day," said Skaald, looking at his Warhammer with the look of nostalgia on his face.

"Are any of the people that could beat you still alive from your old guild," asked Clyde as he was warming up.

"I haven't heard from my guild mates in a few decades. Since I lost a bet and quit the guild anyway... a few came to my shop to make requests but it's hard to say if any of them are around these days."
"What kind of bet did you lose," asked Clyde as he finally got some of Skaald's story to come out.

"Well, there was a rumor going around the guild that there was someone in the town we were staying in that could beat me in a fight. At the time, the big fighters were at the main guild, and I was the strongest in town at the time and it kinda went to my head a bit. I said to bring 'em on if they think they can win. (Hee, hee) You would never guess who they brought to me," said Skaald laughingly.

"It was none other than Skye. They brought her all chained up and upset. Back then, she definitely wasn't as nice as she is now. I've tamed her up quite well. She was still as smart as ever and she already knew Dwarvish when I met her. She looked me over and said, 'You look like a betting man. Let's make a deal.' I told her I'd listen, and she proposed that we fight and if she won, I had to let her go and quit the guild. And I said if I won, she had to join up with us.... I woke up three days later and still couldn't walk for a week... When it was time for the guild to move on, I just told them to leave me," Skaald continued.

Clyde simply looked at Skaald with curiosity and wondered to himself just how strong Skye was.

"After I could walk again, I found Skye and after about five years of trying, I finally wore her down enough to marry me. I only took a few more beatings from her before she gave in (ha, ha, ha)," Skaald finished with a hearty laugh.

"Now, are we gonna talk all evening or are you going to show me if you've improved," said Skaald, breaking the subject.

"Right, on your mark," replied Clyde, preparing himself.

As soon as the fight began, Skaald made a strained fist with his free hand lifting it up causing three large chunks of earth to lift out of the ground. Once they were floating in the air, he took his Warhammer and hit the chunks one after the other sending them at a dangerous speed toward Clyde who was able to dodge them somewhat gracefully. As soon as the last one flew past Clyde, he sprinted right for Skaald to close the distance. He took a few steps and saw Skaald move his hand to the left and expecting the ground to move, Clyde tried to adjust his footing to accommodate. But after Clyde had braced himself, the ground didn't move. Almost before Clyde could react, an earthen spike shot up on his right side which he barely avoided. Clyde then made his way closer to Skaald dodging spikes and staying on his feet from the ground being swept out from under him. Right before he was within striking distance of Skaald, he was caught in a moving earth spell and was heading to meet the ground. Clyde then shoved his spear, lodging it in the ground allowing himself to swing around and deliver a powerful kick toward Skaald's face which was easily blocked with the handle of Skaald's Warhammer. Clyde quickly retracted his leg and swung his sword spear as hard as he could, hearing nothing but the sound of metal meeting metal as Skaald blocked his attack. Clyde was far from finished as he used the momentum to deliver attacks from every open angle he could see, making Skaald unable to cast any spells. Clyde waited patiently for an opening in Skaald's defense while he pounded away. Skaald eventually was forced to take a step back giving Clyde a slim chance to turn the tides. As soon as one of Skaald's legs left the ground, Clyde kicked the back of the weight bearing knee successfully forcing Skaald to the ground with a forceful push from Clyde. Skaald's back hit the ground and before he could make any sort of counter, he noticed Clyde's spear at his throat.

"I yield. I yield. You've bested me, boy," said Skaald, noticeably out of breath from their fight.

Clyde snapped out of his fighting mode and realized that he had in fact won. He couldn't help but show on his face that he was happy with his progress as he helped Skaald off the ground.

"For you to improve this much in only a few days of practice is impressive. I truly wasn't holding back this go around either..." said Skaald as he thought out loud.

"Well, once I figured out how your faster magic was directed, it made it somewhat easier for me to predict which way to expect the attack to come from so it was easier to avoid," explained Clyde.

"I see... Well, I wouldn't fully rely on that for every fight because everyone's skill level with magic is different as well as the different types of magic use different ways other than the hand to perform," explained Skaald as he began to fix the yard.

"You really made a mess of our yard today," said Skye, coming outside to fetch some water.

"I gave him everything I had, and the boy came out on top... He might be able to beat you in a fight dear..." Skaald said as the ground slowly became level again.

"Would you be willing to spar with me now, Skye," asked Clyde, wanting to challenge himself a bit further.

"I...I don't want to..." she said, obviously lying.

"Come on. Fight the boy. I know you don't want anyone to see you when you're in the mood to fight but you should know you won't scare him off so easily," said Skaald talking her into complying.

"F... fine. I'll fight you twice and that's all. If you can't beat me the second time, that's on you," warned Skye as she pretended to be upset.

Clyde ran over to give Skye a reassuring hug as thanks which she seemed surprised and happy about.

"Well, if you're that excited about it, then get ready. I'll be back out in a minute," she said as she ran back into the house.

"You keep doing that, boy, and she won't ever let ya go anywhere (ha, ha)," said Skaald laughingly.

"Guess I'd better get ready. You got any tips on fighting her," asked Clyde beginning to get a bit excited about how strong Skye might actually be.

"Well, she's a lot faster than I am and I wouldn't let any of her lightning spells connect if possible... She doesn't use much ranged magic like me so definitely try to be on your toes," he said as he put the finishing touches on the yard.

Skye came back outside wearing a type of corset that seemed to be used to compress her chest, probably to make her a smaller target of sorts followed by tight leather trousers that had a connecting strap around the base of her feet. Although the outfit was simple, it seemed well thought out to express how Skaald explained she fights. The claws on her hands and feet were exposed and there was no excess clothing to get in the way or hinder her ability to use them. Her tail was also fully exposed, hinting to Clyde that it may not be just for show. Despite Clyde noticing the practicality of her outfit, he couldn't help but notice that it complemented her well, almost as well as the various dresses she normally wears. Her scales seemed to somewhat glow in the sunlight, and as she stretched and began to warm up, Clyde noticed that she had a very toned body that suited a fighter. He began to wonder how she kept in fighting shape when he never sees her train or do anything that came close to it. He also began to worry how right Skaald was about her fighting ability.

"Well... are you ready," she asked as Clyde came back from his thoughts.

"Y...yea, whenever you are... Are you not going to use a weapon," asked Clyde as he watched her scratch the dirt with her foot.

"No, I find it more trouble than it's worth to use one. I can do just fine without," she said confidently as she stretched a final stretch.

"Well, in that case..." Clyde stuck his spear into the ground and proceeded to take his kukri and sword off his waist.

"What are you doing," asked Skye, seemingly confused.

"Well, if you're not using any weapons, I don't see how it's fair for me to. Besides, if I'm going to learn, I might as well try to learn on similar footing," Clyde explained as he threw his blades aside.

Although Clyde knew his way around knives and swords well, he was somewhat better at hand-to-hand fighting, which was the first thing his dad ever taught him. He never really studied a specific martial art; instead, he learned a mixture of them that were very practical in normal fights so he was curious if they would be as useful in this fight.

"Well, if that's what you want..." Skye said before she leaned down on all fours close to the ground.

As soon as she made eye contact with Clyde, her aura completely changed. The only feeling he could read off of her was that he was now her prey. Clyde shook his head, clearing his mind; he couldn't let that sway his determination as he got into a defensive stance and prepared for her to make a move.

"Begin," yelled Skaald as he quickly backed away.

No sooner than he had said it, Skye made her move. Just like lightning, she came after Clyde and was face to face in no time at all. She made a jab straight for Clyde's gut; however, Clyde successfully grabbed her hand and managed to use her momentum to fling her over his shoulder. As she was falling to the ground, she managed to use her tail to maneuver her body, so her feet hit the ground. Clyde wanted to believe he pulled that off on purpose but in truth, it was purely instinct as he wasn't ready for how fast Skye really was but now, he was properly on guard for her. As soon as her feet hit the ground, she was right back on Clyde almost as if she was expecting him to do that. She swung her claw towards Clyde as he blocked it with his arm. His vambrace managed to block all but two of her claws. Unbeknownst to Clyde, they dug deep into his arm. He had no time to realize this as she made another thrust toward Clyde's chest which he deflected with his free arm, pushing Skye to one side of him. Before Clyde could use this opening he created to land a hit of his own, he got smacked hard in the side by Skye's tail kicking him a few feet away. Clyde jumped back to his feet as soon as he stopped sliding across the ground and had only a second to breathe because Skye was on her way to close the distance yet again. *If I can bait her to use her tail one more time, I might be able to create an opening,* Clyde thought as she came right for him staying low to the ground this time. She grabbed Clyde's leg before he realized it and flung him across the yard like he was a small stone, but he landed on his feet somehow and despite Skye being right on him yet again, he went for an attack.

As soon as she hit the ground, Clyde proceeded to pin her in a choke hold. Unfortunately, it didn't last long as Clyde had forgotten about her tail. Once she came back to her senses, she knocked Clyde off with ease... Clyde was able to dodge and get in a position for her to hit him with her tail which she promptly did. As her heavy tail slammed into Clyde's side, he clutched onto it with all his strength and once he knew he had it, he jumped and kicked her in the back, bringing her to the ground. As soon as she hit the ground, Clyde proceeded to pin her in a choke hold; however, he ignorantly forgot about her tail and once she came back to her senses, she easily knocked Clyde off. Before he could get up, she put her foot on his chest dropping him back to the ground.

"Oof... yea.... I yield...you can get off me now..." said Clyde, straining for a full breath of air.

Skye's serious expression lightened up and she seemed to snap back into her normal personality.

"Oh, my goodness. I didn't mean to go so far a..."

Clyde cut her off quickly as he raised his hand to stop her from continuing.

"I'm fine but I wish you wouldn't have held back like you did. I appreciate that you care about me but if I get in a real fight like this, I'm afraid I won't be as lucky every time. So, once I'm healed up and practice a bit more, I'll take my second fight with you but only if you go all out," said Clyde, heavily wondering and hoping Skye doesn't take it the wrong way.

"So, you're not scared of me after seeing me like that," she asked weakly.

Clyde couldn't help but have a confused expression written all over him as he answered her.

"Why would I be scared of you? You've just shown me how strong you really are inside," said Clyde as he struggled to his feet hiding his bleeding arm from Skye.

"Inside," she asked as she dusted Clyde off.

"You have strength, there's no question about that. What I'm trying to say is that your strength is more than physical. You are stronger than anyone I know simply because you restrain yourself and don't fall to the temptation of using that strength to get your way," Clyde explained as he headed over to pick his weapons up.

Skye simply blushed as her face turned purple and she smiled and went inside the house. Skaald walked over to Clyde laying his hand on his shoulder.

"You done well, boy, but do you really think you can beat her without your weapons," he asked as he used a cloth he had for sweat to wrap Clyde's bleeding arm after he took his vambrace off.

"I feel like I definitely could if she chooses not to use her magic like she did this time. (Ahh) Unfortunately, I'm not sure how much her magic will help her fighting so I suppose it'll be a mystery," explained Clyde as the salty sweat- covered cloth stung his wound.

"It looked to me like you were having trouble keeping up with her... like most people that's fought her. How are you going to compensate for that," Skaald said tying the bandage tight.

"Well, although she's faster, she slows down a bit when she actually attacks enough to where if I quit overthinking, I can probably get a few lucky grapples in like I did at the first of the fight to throw her off guard... even if it's for just a second." Clyde was running the scenarios through his mind making him almost unbearably excited for his rematch.

After Skaald patched him up, they went inside. Clyde spent the rest of the day somewhat meditating and recalling everything he possibly could from what his father taught him.

"If im going to win, I suppose I can't really use normal martial arts in this situation... I'm not fighting a Human which is what martial arts was invented for so I'm going to have to go on instinct and alter my fighting style to be more affective in odd situations like this," said Clyde quietly to himself as he thought.

Once Skye and Skaald went to bed, Clyde used the opportunity to retrieve some herbal medicine from Skye's cabinet in the kitchen to treat his wound. To Clyde's surprise, when he opened the door to leave his room, he saw the medicine he was looking for sitting right outside with a note attached.

("I know you tried to hide it thinking I forgot how badly I hurt your arm but I'm in full control when I fight so I know what I did. This should heal you up nicely and please put a clean bandage on it.")

Clyde couldn't help but feel a bit dumb thinking she hadn't noticed but that knowledge gave him more to think about in terms of his fight with Skye. He brought the medicine to his room and lit some candles. As he unbandaged his wound, the pain came searing to his brain it seemed. Probably because it was wrapped so tightly. After he got the bandage unstuck from his arm, he could properly see just what kind of damage was done. He had two deep puncture wounds on his upper forearm just as he assumed where his armor didn't reach. They were quite painful, but it was mostly due to the tight bandage. Clyde got some water in his bedside pitcher and washed the wound thoroughly even though getting the dirt and dried blood out was painful, he finished it properly. After it was clean, he took a closer look, at least the best he could with candlelight, to try and see if anything important was damaged. Although it was painful to move his fingers, he was still very much able to, and the wound didn't seem to bleed anymore after he cleaned it, so it seemed as though he got lucky. He then began to apply the medicine, which, once it was in his wound, it felt like he had lit it on fire. After some muffled noises of pain, he took a clean rag and wrapped it just tight enough for it to stay on securely. Before Clyde called it a night, he decided to check his armor and see what damage he would have to repair. Surprisingly the only real damage was a few dents in his breastplate and then his vambrace. She had gripped it so tightly that the claws in contact with it almost penetrated completely through which was very surprising to Clyde. For one, if she was holding any of her strength back, thin steel armor was effectively useless if she really wanted to hurt someone. Secondly, if he wasn't wearing his armor, he might have lost the use of his left hand all together, so the next best thing he needed to do was make his armor a bit thicker and possibly re-temper it to make it harder to penetrate.

As he thought everything over, he drifted off to sleep sitting at his little table in his room. The next morning, he was being woken up by none other than Skye as she was inspecting his wound for herself.

"I didn't realize I was gripping your arm so tightly... I suppose I got a little carried away since you were lasting longer than I thought," she said, noticing that Clyde was awake.

"That just tells me that I was doing better than you expected and these new scars will remind me in the future to not be careless," said Clyde as he took his arm away from Skye to stretch and pop his stiff bones from sleeping in a chair.

The next week went by rather quickly as Clyde tweaked his armor to accommodate what he thought he needed. It took him a few days to heal up enough to use his hand properly again, thanks to the medicine Skye provided him. Although it always felt like putting hot coals on his wound, it truly did seem to make it heal faster than just leaving it alone. By the end of the week, it was almost completely closed up and Clyde was back to training. Luckily, Skaald agreed to spar with him more which helped Clyde improve even more by predicting when and where his spells were going to come from and what they were going to be. Unfortunately, Clyde knew that it was only accomplished by reading Skaald specifically and wouldn't necessarily apply to every mage he would encounter but he was sure it would help. At the beginning of the following week, he decided to go visit Oliver. He wondered if there was any way he could use magic to fight.

He made his way to the sketchy-looking house and knocked loudly on the door. Clyde waited patiently for Oliver to peek out and see who it was. After a few more minutes, Clyde decided to bang on the door louder and was met by an ill response.

"If you bang on that door one more time before I get there, I'll…. Oh, it's you… Well, what are you standing around for? Come on in," said Oliver after he realized his guest was a friend.

Clyde couldn't help but smile at the hateful old goat as he followed him inside listening to his angry rambling.

"The other day, these darn kids came by thinking this was some haunted house making one of the little ones walk up to the porch. I used a little rain spell to drench the little rats and scared them all off. (hee, hee.) What have you been up to," Oliver asked as he stopped at his favorite chair and sat down.

"Well, I've been doing a bit of training involving magic and I was wondering if you could help me out with it," asked Clyde, hoping to get things to the point.

"You figured out how to use magic," he said surprised.

"Well, no, but I have been learning how it works in combat, and I figured you might could show me what you know."

"Well, if that's the case, I may be able to help you; however, I'll have an unfair advantage, if you're alright with that," said Oliver as he strained to get out of his chair.

"What do you mean by that," asked Clyde as he watched the old man get his body ready.

"Well, it's simple, I'm a long-range mage so I need someone to do the upfront fighting for me," he explained as he made his way to the courtyard.

The house was surprisingly large and surrounded a courtyard that lay in the middle of the house where it was obvious that he practiced his magic.

"Who's going to fight for you," Clyde asked, wondering if there was another person living with him.

"Well, you have the choice look over here. Pick whichever one you prefer," Oliver said as he pointed at three statues lined up in the courtyard.

"First, we have Rock. He's quite slow but very durable and strong," explained Oliver as he introduced the largest of the statues. It resembled an orc or ogre of some sorts and was easily ten foot tall.

"Secondly is Roger. He's more of a brawler. He can probably hold you off well," Oliver said pointing at the second one who was about the size of a large Human.

"And lastly, we have Zoom. He's built for speed and honestly my most troublesome one to fight," Oliver said as he pointed to the slender almost snake-like statue.

"So, which one would you like to face along with me? I'll let you know that you will be victorious if you can touch me before you yield or are unable to fight," explained Oliver.

"Sounds good to me... but what exactly are these things," asked Clyde, before he had to choose.

"Oh, these are Golems. They're little side projects of mine," explained Oliver as he began inspecting them for something.

"Golems... I thought enchanting was illegal. Isn't that basically what Golems are," asked Clyde curiously.

"No, no, it's not necessarily enchanting. Golem creating is more or less considered its own magic in a way. Enchanting is placing a certain spell on an object that is to be activated by using a small amount of one's magic later. A Golem is the art of breathing life into a certain object or creation. The reason enchanting is illegal is because of how unbalanced it made things in war and such a level one could have access to level five magic with ease which obviously was extremely dangerous in some cases. Golems, on the other hand, take months to perfect and are nowhere near as powerful in most cases. So that's the main difference."

"I see. How interesting... Well, I choose the fast one to fight," said Clyde knowing that it was good practice for fighting Skye.

"Very well," said Oliver as he laid his hand over the Golem's face.

In an instant, the eyes of the Golem began to glow a bright purple, and the color of its skin began to change to a more natural look almost as if Clyde was going to fight a real oddly shaped Human. Its stiff joints began to articulate and began to move with ease as it stepped down from its pedestal.

"Alright Zoom, get prepared for battle," said Oliver to the now fully awakened Golem.

It simply nodded in response as it began stretching or perhaps testing its limbs to make sure they were ready to go. Oliver began walking to the far side of the courtyard and once he got in position, the Golem finished whatever it was doing and gave Oliver a nod.

"Are you ready, Clyde," asked Oliver as he was taking his encumbering robe off revealing pants and a simple cloth tunic underneath.

Clyde drew his sword and put on his helmet before answering Oliver.

"Ready when you are old man," yelled Clyde as he took a fighting stance watching the Golem in front of him who was in turn watching Oliver awaiting its next order.

Clyde took a small moment to consider his options. Depending on how strong the Golem was, his best option would be to rush straight for Oliver and end the fight before too many spells were shot off. If the Golem was relative in strength to Skaald or Skye, he would have to swap priorities and deal with the Golem while dodging or blocking the incoming magic.

"Begin," yelled Oliver and not a second after, the Golem turned to face Clyde.

Clyde was ready and waiting when the Golem sprinted towards him making a wide, easily dodged swing towards Clyde. Although the Golem was fast, it didn't seem to be able to match Skye's combat speed which made this opening attack easy for Clyde to dodge. When he did, the Golem was wide open for Clyde to make a deep slash with his sword which he promptly took. Oddly, the blade seemed to pass through the Golem far too easily. Once Clyde finished the cut and repositioned himself to prepare for what the Golem may do next, he noticed that his strike didn't seem to have any noticeable effect on the Golem's body. As Clyde was lost in thought, he got hit by what felt like a boulder coming from the direction that Oliver was in. Clyde slid a few feet but managed to keep his balance. Clyde glanced over toward Oliver and figured since he didn't see anything, it must have been wind magic which explained why Skaald said it was difficult to avoid. Clyde noticed that Oliver seemed to be preparing another spell but out of the corner of his eye the Golem sprinted toward him for another assault. Clyde used his sword and deflected the blow successfully to his surprise. *He's weaker than I thought but I think a direct attack would probably still put me down,* Clyde thought while he was under the Golem preparing to slide through it again. Before he could, the belly of the Golem burst open as if it had been shot with a gun and another burst of air hit Clyde. It was weakened from going through the Golem, making the impact bearable. Clyde's earlier suspicion was confirmed when globs of the Golem were all over Clyde. Now, he got out from under the Golem and made a bit of distance so he could think. The Golem was apparently made out of some kind of liquid which is why his sword was so useless against it. Unfortunately, that's all Clyde had time to think since the Golem was recovered and dashing toward him yet again. At this point, Clyde then made a turning point decision. He couldn't afford to keep losing the first time he fought something new and thinking about things slowed him down too much. So, after a quick breath, Clyde cleared his mind and simply relied on his instinct and training, not only from his father but his new friends as well. The Golem went for a quick barrage of attacks once it was within range and Clyde blocked and dodged everyone that came his way. Soon after, another burst of air came through the

Golem which Clyde was able to avoid and taking the opportunity since the Golem was stunned, he ran past the Golem straight for Oliver. Clyde saw Oliver motion his hands presumably in preparation for another spell. Clyde tried to dodge it by straying to the side, but the wind spell caught his shoulder, spinning Clyde sideways giving him a chance to glance at the Golem which was already on top of Clyde about to attack. A loud bang sounded as Clyde couldn't get his guard up in time to avoid its attack and it hit him square in the chest ringing off of his armor knocking Clyde to the ground. No sooner than Clyde realized he was on the ground did the Golem continue its assault thrashing its arms as if they were large heavy whips. Clyde was able to deflect them and found a small break in the Golem's assault to get back to his feet. After Clyde and the Golem went at it for a moment longer as Clyde deflected and sliced aimlessly at the Golem, suddenly it jumped back out of Clyde's reach. Clyde instantly looked towards Oliver's direction as a large slow ball of fire was coming towards him. Clyde could feel the intense heat from the flame almost as if he were standing in front of a bonfire and all of a sudden, the flame went from a golden crimson to a deep blue as it increased in speed drastically and instantly became unbearably hot. Clyde leapt out of the way of the impact area and as soon as the flame hit the ground it erupted as tiny particles of flame shot out in every direction. Clyde didn't waste time to be intimidated by the magic and he took the opportunity to close more distance between him and Oliver. Clyde noticed that Oliver seemed to be tired from using a flashy spell and was struggling to make his next one as Clyde got within striking distance of Oliver. He quickly clasped his hands together causing a dome of wind to form around him blowing Clyde back almost ten feet away. Clyde landed on his feet when the wind stopped and he heard the Golem closing in behind him, so Clyde unsheathed his kukri and threw it, landing it precisely beside Oliver's foot. Seeing this, Oliver smiled and snapped his fingers stopping the Golem's assault.

"Well, I'm lucky you weren't aiming to kill now, aren't I," asked Oliver as he wiped the sweat from his brow and sat on the ground.

"I still don't think I've properly won," said Clyde as he approached Oliver and sat beside him.

"Whatever makes you say that," asked Oliver as he looked questioningly at Clyde.

"I had no chance against that Golem... even if I killed you, it wouldn't have stopped until I destroyed its core, right," asked Clyde as he jerked his kukri out of the ground.

"True enough, but as far as your intended training, I believe you did quite well... Despite not having any magic, not only did you survive my Golem, but you managed to survive while a mage was targeting you which is impressive for most people that can actually use magic," explained Oliver as he patted Clyde's shoulder.

"Besides, there aren't many Golem makers around anymore so they're not as common as you might think, especially battle-ready ones like these... Most Golems are made to help with chores or farming. Also, as far as mages like me, the only thing I can tell you is that if you fight a stronger or younger one, they may use weaker quicker spells, but you seem quite adaptable when it comes to speed."

"I see. Well, I appreciate you taking the time to spar with me Oliver. I'll bring you some dinner in a day or so as thanks," said Clyde as he got up from the ground and helped Oliver up shortly after.

"You'd best not slouch on the meat then. I'll expect it to be good too, " said Oliver as he led Clyde to the door.

"Of course. I'm sure they've got plenty of pickled pigs' feet this time of year," said Clyde jokingly.

"If you bring me pigs' feet, then you'll think a Golem's hard to kill when all three come after you," said Oliver as he slammed the door behind Clyde. He couldn't quite tell if he was joking or not.

After a few days of rest and owning up to some promises, Clyde was feeling ready for his rematch with Skye.

"You think you can win this time," asked Oliver, who was enjoying his hearty stew Clyde had brought him.

"I think I can. At least last long enough to say I gave her a challenge... As far as actually beating her, I'll just have to hope I get lucky," said Clyde, trying not to think too much about the upcoming fight.

"Just trust yourself. I'm sure you can fight better than you think," complimented Oliver as he finished the big bowl of stew.

Clyde shortly left and headed towards the forge where Skye and Skaald awaited him. Skye was already warming up in her fighting apparel.

"Well, you'd best get ready. If you take too long, you'll be doing the dishes after our fight," joked Skye as she saw Clyde walk up.

"Actually... I have a favor to ask you Skye," said Clyde.

"Oh? What is it?"

"Well, I don't want you to hold back like you did last time," said Clyde as he somehow felt bad having to ask her.

"I see... So, you knew...," said Skye quietly.

"Well, it wasn't hard to tell that you were holding back, especially from the stories Skaald has told me."

Skye looked over at Skaald with quite a mean expression.

"W...what? You expect me not to brag about my wife," Skaald said defensively.

Skye sighed a deep sigh as she looked back at Clyde.

"If I do, you'd best promise you'll give up before I hurt you.... I tend to get carried away a bit when I fight, especially when I don't hold myself back," she said with a worried expression.

"Well, I'd rather let you beat me senseless so I can learn my limits rather than learn them from fighting something that wants to kill me," said Clyde with a smile.

His answer seemed to satisfy Skye as she smiled at him and motioned him to go get ready, which he did. Clyde returned to the yard with his equipment on and like before, he set his spear and sword to the side before squaring up with Skye.

"Are you sure you don't want to use your weapons," asked Skye, hinting that she thinks Clyde needs them.

"Like I said before, it's only fair if I use hand-to-hand as well," said Clyde, smiling at Skye.

"Very well... prepare yourself," she said as she changed her expression to her cold hunting stare.

Unlike last time, Clyde wouldn't let her gaze shake him. He simply prepared for her fast first strike. Clyde readied himself and took a long deep breath clearing his mind of useless thoughts. He decided that this time had to be different. Skye was far too fast for him to try to calculate any sort of plan or strategy, and it was best for him to simply do like he did against Oliver and only focus on one thing: Surviving long enough to win.

"Begin," shouted Skaald as he quickly got himself out of the way.

Skye shot toward Clyde like a bolt of lightning, staying close to the ground as she began to deliver a sweeping kick at Clyde's feet. Clyde simply jumped to avoid it and before he even touched the ground, Skye had repositioned herself and was aiming a strong kick toward Clyde's side. Luckily, he was able to raise his leg enough to block her powerful kick that sent Clyde a few feet in the opposite direction before he hit the ground. Clyde was quickly able to get back to his feet and as soon as his feet hit the ground, Skye was already right on him with a slash coming his him. It was fast but it was a wide-open opportunity for Clyde to counter, which he took quickly. He grabbed her arm just before she was able to follow through and he used her momentum to pin her arm around her back. Her tail was coming to knock Clyde away, but the same trick wasn't going to work twice. So, he grabbed her tail with his free hand and leg right as it slammed into his side successfully immobilizing it. Just as Clyde was about to kick the back of her knee to bring Skye to the ground, Clyde felt every hair on his body stick straight up. Clyde let go of his captive and jumped back just as Skye's body discharged sparks of electricity in every direction. Clyde noticed as soon as the sparks dissipated into the ground that Skye shook her body like a wet dog. For some reason, he thought that maybe that affected her too in a way. His thought wouldn't last long as Skye turned toward Clyde and looked ready for her next attack. Skye then held her hand out toward Clyde and a ball of water formed almost instantly. Clyde was prepared to dodge it when it burst into a mist that instantly surrounded Clyde. As soon as Clyde saw the mist, he kneeled on the ground grabbing his metal greaves just in time to see Skye's body surrounded in sparks right before she launched a stream of lightning toward Clyde turning the mist into smoke as it traveled and surrounded Clyde. Luckily, Clyde saw the lightning coming and he had successfully grounded himself properly enough that the lightning only barely tingled as it made its way into the earth. As soon as the lightning dissipated, he sprinted toward Skye who was shaking off the lightning as she did before. Clyde caught Skye off guard as he tackled her to the ground. Clyde straddled himself on top of Skye and before she had a chance to break free, Clyde drew a knife he had in his boot and put it to her throat. Skye, after noticing the knife, only smiled kindly at Clyde.

"I yield... You've bested me," Skye said softly.

Clyde let out a big relieving sigh as he threw the knife to the side. And before he could get off Skye, she grabbed his shoulders and got up, lifting Clyde as if he were a child.

"Wha... wait a minute," said Clyde alarmingly before Skye sat him down and embraced him in a warm hug.

"I suppose you're ready for what this world may throw at you. We've taught you everything we know to teach you," Skye said as she began to cry.

"Hey now... you're making it sound like I'm leaving or something. Y...you don't have to cry...," said Clyde while he was being squeezed by Skye.

Skaald laid his hand on Clyde's shoulder while he was being smothered by Skye.

"Well, we thought that's why you wanted us to teach you all this, so you could go adventuring and figure out how you got here and all," explained Skaald.

"Well, I am planning on leaving eventually but I've still got some things to do before I go, unless you guys are just gonna kick me out now," said Clyde, trying to lighten the mood.

"So, you're staying for a bit longer," asked Skye as she loosened her grip on Clyde.

"Yea, I'll stay until I have enough money saved up to comfortably travel to where I need to. Plus, I still plan on hunting a Gex before I go as well," said Clyde, reassuring Skye.

Clyde couldn't help but be surprised that Skye broke down just because she thought he was leaving, which left Clyde with a heavy heart. Clyde knew that eventually he needed to move on and begin searching for the reason he's in this world. He also knew that if he decided to give up on his precious life all together, he knew where he would feel welcome and at home.

"Hey…," Clyde said getting Skye and Skaald's attention before they headed inside.

"Yea, what is it, boy," said Skaald with a rough smile.

"Th... thanks for being so kind to me all this time... You... you've really made me feel at home here," confessed Clyde, not being able to look at either of them.

"Well, we should thank you for giving us something we could never have on our own...," said Skaald, scratching his head as he and Skye looked at each other.

"But that's enough of that talk. You'd best get in here and clean yourself up before supper," Skaald said, changing the subject.

Clyde simply smiled and followed behind them as soon as he grabbed his things.

Chapter 5: The Hunt

The next day, Clyde was in more pain than he originally thought he would be. His side that took the force of Skye's tail when he caught it was bruised quite badly. Luckily though, Clyde couldn't feel where he had broken anything and his leg that blocked Skye's kick was in roughly the same condition, as he could barely stand on it from the pain. Clyde didn't realize just how much of a beating he took from just two solid hits from Skye. Thinking back on his fight, he couldn't really see a better outcome though. Despite trying, Clyde couldn't hide the fact that he was in pain and Skye could tell as soon as she laid eyes on Clyde, which meant that Clyde was forced to rest for a couple days as Skye tended to his bruises with some of her miracle ointment. Clyde made sure to make Skye show him how to make it and surprisingly it was one of the simpler things she had taught him to make. The only downside was that the ingredients were difficult to obtain in the wild and quite a chore to keep in her garden. She told Clyde that on everyone else, the wounds heal almost twice as fast as it did on Clyde. Only Clyde knew that it actually made him heal a lot faster than any remedies he knew of from his old world. Over those couple days where Skye wouldn't let Clyde do much, he picked her brain about the medicine as well as a few other ointments and things she had taught him. He learned that he could make the medicine using a few different ingredients depending on where he was which he diligently described the alternative plants as best he could in his notebook which would no doubt come in handy.

It took nearly three whole days before Skye was satisfied with Clyde's recovery enough for him to begin his preparations for his hunt. He immediately went to Darren's so he could order the necessary supplies.

"Yes sir, that will be three and one sixth gold neros," said Darren, talking to an older traveler.

"That's outrageous! I'll give you two and a half and that's all," said the old man, clearly frustrated with Darren's offer.

"The best I can do is three," said Darren, unshaken by the man's frustration.

After the man scratched his beard for a moment, he grumbled as he stretched his hand out to confirm the deal with Darren.

"The more I come to this town, the more I hate buying supplies from a young pup like you," grumbled the old man as he handed Darren the coins.

"Your business is always appreciated, Guss," Darren said, sending the old traveler on his way.

"You've definitely got the talent for this," Clyde said as Darren finally concluded his business.

"Well, you learn after the first few times you let people bring your price too low and you can't afford to eat the next day," said Darren, cutting a slice of cheese he had stacked behind the counter and throwing Clyde a piece.

"I suppose that definitely makes a difference... Did you lose any money on that deal," asked Clyde curiously.

"Normally that would be quite rude to ask," Darren said as he ate a piece of cheese.

"Normally a friend wouldn't hesitate to explain an accomplishment to his friend," Clyde shot back.

"Oh, your words truly move me," said Darren as if he were acting a part out in a play.

"Truly though, I made quite the profit off of that transaction," said Darren after his performance.

"Oh? How so?"

"Well, that man specifically comes to town twice a year and gets supplies to get him to some place he goes to in the south. He's a merchant, not just a simple traveler, which I mistook the first few times I'd met him. He buys supplies here and sells them to some villages in the south for quite a profit. And normally the supplies I sold him would be worth closer to two gold rather than three but he's making such a profit down south, he can't really afford to change his route just to buy from someone else, so I keep the price fairly high," explained Darren.

"Hmm, I see. Isn't the big town to the south more convenient to buy stuff from," asked Clyde.

"The town to the south is a large trading hub so unless he's making a significantly larger purchase, the trade taxes will hurt his profits quite a bit. Even for a normal traveler, you're better off buying supplies from surrounding villages rather than a large town or city due to the taxes for unregistered merchants."

"I see... how interesting," said Clyde, processing the information.

"Well, on another note, how about you tell me how your training is going," said Darren, breaking the silence.

"Well... I suppose it was successful although I feel like I didn't make much progress," said Clyde reluctantly.

"What? Couldn't you win against Skye?"

"I did, but not fairly," explained Clyde.

"Ahh, well then, what's your next goal?"

"I plan to hunt a Gex and kill one," said Clyde plainly.

A moment went by as Darren simply looked at Clyde seeming to expect something else.

"Y... you're serious," said Darren when he realized Clyde wasn't telling a joke.

"Of course. If im going to prove whether or not my training has paid off, I need to out hunt the hunter."

"I'm sure you don't need me to tell you how insane that logic is. Do you even have a plan," asked a now concerned Darren.

"I'll come up with something, I'm sure. But for now, I just need to pick up some supplies."

"Supplies?... Well, you do have some credit with me still but what all do you need," asked Darren as he switched gears back into merchant mode.

"I'll need everything on this list. By tomorrow, if possible," said Clyde as he handed over the parchment.

"Hmm. I'm afraid you can't afford the salt... but everything else seems achievable by tomorrow," Darren said as he scanned the list.

"I'm sure you can part with that meager amount of salt until I return to pay you."

"With your suicidal quest in mind, Im not sure I should risk the loss. Salt isn't necessarily cheap, even a small bag. It's hard to come by around here," Darren said quite seriously.

"Although it may not be cheap, it's not like it's going to ruin your business if I don't make it back."

"Fine, I'll get you the salt... When you get back, I'll expect you to pay me double its worth," said an irritated Darren.

"Alright, we'll see. I appreciate it," said Clyde as he began to leave the shop.

"Hey…. I'll be expecting you to return, ya know? You're not allowed to die with debt," joked Darren, wishing Clyde good luck in his own way.

Clyde simply waved at him as he left to head back to the forge. Once he got back, he noticed Skye working on her medicines at her small workstation. "Would you like some help," asked Clyde as he approached Skye.

"Absolutely! Come grab a mortar... I've wanted to talk to you anyways," said Skye excitedly as Clyde sat down beside her and began grinding up herbs.

After Clyde and Skye worked in silence for a time, Clyde finally spoke up.

"So, what is it you wanted to talk about," asked Clyde as he grinded intently on the herbs.

"Well.... are you sure you have to do this? I mean do you have a reason to actually hunt one or what," asked Skye, with worry in her voice.

Clyde didn't really have an answer for her because he didn't really have an answer for himself. He paused for quite a while until Skye began talking again, bringing him back from his thoughts.

"So, you don't have an answer, do you? I figured as much," she said as she placed her hand on Clyde's shoulder.

"It's okay to not have a reason to achieve a goal that you set for yourself. Sometimes it makes reaching the goal easier if you're not pushing yourself for some self-centered reason... Honestly, even though I wish you would just drop it and do something else, I have to admit that you should be ready to achieve this goal of yours."

"Well, sorry I don't have some grand reason as to why I want to do this, but it does make me feel at ease hearing your confidence in me," said Clyde as he smiled at Skye.

"Well, I suppose since I've taken such good care of you this far, I had best give you something just in case things don't go necessarily the way you want them to," she said as she grabbed a black wooden box she had next to her.

Skye pulled out a small vial with a long leather string attached to it and handed it to Clyde.

"Put that around your neck and only drink what's inside if you have no other options left... do you understand," said Skye quite seriously.

Clyde took the vial and examined it closely; it couldn't have possibly contained any more than a drop or two of whatever was in it and the liquid itself was almost completely black. The small cork on top was almost too small to take out with fingers but possibly teeth would work. Clyde quit looking at it and put it around his neck as he was told.

"What exactly is it," asked Clyde quite curiously.

"It's something that my people's warriors used as a last resort... it makes your physical limitations disappear for an unknown amount of time; however, the after-effects are uncertain so please listen when I say to use it only if you have no other option," said Skye almost second guessing giving it to Clyde.

Clyde took a moment to re-examine the small vial again.

"Why are you giving me something so precious to your people?"

At this question, Skye seemed unable to look at Clyde directly while she answered.

"B... because I care about you and I want to make sure you'll make it back home," she said as her face began to glow a shade of purple.

"I wish you wouldn't worry about me so... but I can't help but feel happy that you do," said Clyde before he gave Skye a much-needed hug.

Afterwards they began working again on Skye's orders.

"Don't worry too much. I'll be back one way or another."

"Well, if you make it back without using that vial, I'll teach you how to make it. It takes almost two months to make that small amount.... Also, the ingredients are hard to come by and quite expensive to buy," explained Skye, trying to give Clyde more of a reason to come back.

"I'll look forward to learning it from you."

They continued working till the candles burned out and they went off to bed.

The next day, Clyde woke up early and began his final preparations for his hunt. He made his way to Darren's and collected his provisions as well as a hand cart and made his way back to the forge where he finished packing what he needed and began putting his armor back on after he had mended it from his previous fights.

"You have everything you need? Are you taking enough food? Don't you think you might need more," said Skye as she was circling Clyde's cart.

"I'm sure I've got everything. Don't you worry," said Clyde as he finished putting his armor on.

"Don't you wanna just stay one more night and rest before you go?"

"Now you know better than that, dear," interrupted Skaald, saving Clyde from having to escape Skye's begging.

"I'd best be off. I'd like to find a good spot to set up by tomorrow morning," said Clyde as he hurriedly picked the rest of his things up and began pulling the handcart along.

The town was out of Clyde's sight within an hour of walking. Clyde sighed a deep sigh after he escaped all the excitement. He was thinking of how much more cumbersome bringing the handcart along was being and he thought that it was slowing down his traveling speed significantly.

"Well, the bright side is, I won't be struggling out here with all the equipment I've brought along," he said to himself.

He then began thinking of how he was going to successfully hunt his prey. He thought he could realistically accomplish his goal one way: he had to find a way to not only lure but separate one from the group since he's only seen them in sets of two whenever they're hunting. He was going to have to watch them more in order to be able to figure out what he needed to do to capture one.

Clyde walked all day and a few hours into the night seeing that the moon was full, and he could still see fairly well before he decided to set up camp. He had decided that this would be his little base camp for now since it wasn't on the main trail of the Tork or Gex, and also was near a freshwater source. After a mostly sleepless night, Clyde went to the large valley and climbed up the cliff side to the plateau to begin his search for the Tork and Gex.

Clyde's tracked and searched for almost a week and a half before he had finally found the Tork herd. Unfortunately, the herd was almost a day's walk from Clyde's base camp. The direction in which they were slowly grazing toward was closer to where Clyde wanted them to be, which would give Clyde maybe two days to observe and come up with a plan to capture a Gex by using possibly a Tork as bait. He watched patiently as the Tork slowly grazed along looking for anything he could use to capture one or even witness the Gex hunt. A day and a half passed and there was still no sign of any Gex to be found. The Tork were moving far slower than Clyde had anticipated so realistically he was looking at another four days before they got close to where Clyde had planned to capture one. Clyde noticed that there were particular berry bushes that the Tork very much enjoyed eating over their normal diet and there were clusters of them scattered all about the land and Clyde could easily drug one of them to make the Tork easier to handle and capture. Just as he was thinking about how he could do that; he noticed off in the distance there was smoke coming from beyond the next ridge.

"Surely there's not another group of people trying to travel through here," Clyde said to himself.

Clyde pondered on it for a bit and decided he might as well take a look since he had plenty of time to spare. Despite seeing the smoke just over the ridge, it took Clyde nearly half a day to make it up said ridge in order to check out the source of the smoke. Clyde's suspicion was confirmed as there was nearly a group of seven to ten people setting up camp in the valley. Clyde took a long scan of the surrounding area, and another question was quickly answered as he spotted a Gex watching them from a nearby cliff. This Gex in particular seemed different. Clyde could tell at a distance that its color was faded, and it just had a different posture about it all together than the one he had fought. As Clyde was quietly observing it, it seemed to have spotted Clyde and looked for a good minute before it descended from the cliff it was on and disappeared from Clyde's site. Clyde took a moment to decide on what he should do, and he knew if he didn't help them, they would be slaughtered that night. Although Clyde wasn't certain he could stop it from happening either, even if he did help. Clyde's base camp was too far away to retrieve any supplies so Clyde would have to make do with what he currently had on him which included his weapons and food and water. Clyde heavily considered his decision, but he then began to think of what Skye would do in his shoes. Then with a heavy sigh, he got up and began to make his way down to the camp.

Clyde literally walked into their camp and was almost in the center before he was even noticed by anyone.

"H... hey, who are you!! Stop where you are," shouted a familiar voice.

Clyde turned toward the man, and he almost completely regretted his decision upon seeing who it was. It was the same person that he had beaten up for disrespecting Skye past the point of tears.

"Wait a minute... you're that lizard lover from that deadbeat town. What are you doing way out here," asked the man in an obviously cocky tone.

"I've come to try and save your lives so long as you don't continue to annoy me," Clyde said, getting to the point.

"We don't need saving. Heck, we've nearly made it all the way through this place."

"What's all this commotion about," said one of the older men that was part of the ones that had beaten Clyde in the alleyway.

"This moron thinks we're in danger, Vice-Captain. He's probably just trying to cover up being some kind of thief or something."

"In danger you say? I remember you. The Captain thought pretty highly of you after our last encounter... I'll hear you out, so please explain," said the Vice-Captain.

"Right... well, you're about to be attacked by a pack of Gex and from my experience, you're more than ill-prepared for such an attack," explained Clyde.

"I see. So, those beasts are real?... Fine. What do you suggest we do," asked the Vice-Captain to Clyde's surprise.

"First you need to gather your people and move out from the open to a more defendable place or at least have some decent lookouts because when they attack, it's fast and precise. Secondly, since you've already been spotted with your fire, you need to light some around the camp for visibility once it gets dark. They like to use the confusion of darkness when they attack," explained Clyde.

"Right. We can't move 'cause we have some sick with us and moving now would make their condition worse.... Hey, you go get the ones searching for food and tell them to bring firewood when they come back, and you wake the morons that's supposed to be on lookout," shouted the Vice-Captain as his men ran to do their respective jobs.

"Now you... tell me how hard these things are to kill," he said, looking at Clyde.

"Their outer shell is stronger than most armor and their arms have something similar to a sword on them that resembles this spear. As far as killing one, you need to aim for the joints or bust through their armor. They're not mindless creatures either; they seem to think and fight just as if they were trained swordsmen, so don't underestimate them in terms of skill and Intelligence. I'm not sure how well magic works against them, so I wouldn't count on it unless you have a strong mage. Also, it would work best if you paired your people up in groups of two or three to avoid them being able to single anyone out. Also, fighting more than one would almost be suicide so it would be best to avoid that, if possible," Clyde explained as carefully as he could the best way he thought they could successfully survive the upcoming attack.

"Right, then let's begin preparations," said the Vice-Captain as he ran to his men.

Clyde helped the group prepare as best he could with what little remaining daylight they had. A proper headcount of everyone able to fight was twenty people and the sick or unable was ten. Clyde and the Vice-Captain thought it best to have the ten who couldn't fight in a single tent in the middle of the formation, surrounding them is five teams of four watching the horizon as the light faded from the sky.

"W... well, it looks as though we're watching each other's back," said the girl to Clyde and the other two guys.

"Hey, don't you worry, Little Pix, you just sit back and let us deal with these monsters," said one of the men obviously trying to impress her.

"From what I recall, you're a mage, correct," asked Clyde, watching as far as the surrounding fire's light would let him.

"Y... yes, I am but I'm not very fast at casting and my spells aren't exactly that strong," said Little Pix nervously.

"What is the best spell you can use most often?"

"Oh... uh, I can launch a small water missile once a minute that's strong enough to knock a horse off its feet," she said quickly.

"Good, as soon as a Gex is spotted, I'll need you to begin your spell and fire it as soon as we create an opening. That could possibly be a life saver," said Clyde

The other two seemed to agree with Clyde and joined him in keeping a strong watch.

Almost three hours after nightfall, everything went eerily quiet. It seemed as though the only thing you could hear was the crackling of the many fires spread throughout the camp. Everything else seemed to have stopped in time. Then all of a sudden, from the darkness, a shadowy figure lunged toward the camp and engaged the group to Clyde's left. Before anyone could properly react, more came busting out from the darkness. Clyde grabbed his spear and with barely enough time, he blocked the Gex's first strike fully. Pain rushed through his hand from the strong force. Clyde managed to stop, and it seemed to have stunned the Gex for a second as well, giving Clyde's group just enough time to quit being surprised and jump into the fight. The Gex quickly recovered and began to strike Clyde with its other arm, but it was successfully stopped by Clyde's comrade. Clyde took the opportunity to take his spear and jam it into the Gex's joint causing it to screech out in pain. Unfortunately, Clyde couldn't get deep enough to kill it, and, in an instant, it recovered and swung its sword arm catching one of the men off guard and split his head in two. Blood shot out in every direction, but Clyde didn't hesitate. He readjusted his grip on his spear and jammed it deep into the Gex finally killing it. They didn't have time to celebrate or mourn because another one that had finished killing its group quickly leapt after Clyde. Clyde tried once to get his spear out of the dead Gex, but it wouldn't come free and right before his new opponent was within range, he drew his sword and deflected its first attack. The other man in his group tried to attack from behind. Unfortunately, though, it seemed like this Gex was more experienced than the previous one and almost without hesitation, it decapitated the man just as he was within its range. Clyde then noticed that it was the same discolored Gex that he had seen the day before and it dawned on him why it was different.

"So, I take it you must be some kinda alpha," Clyde said in-between catching his breath.

Clyde didn't have long to catch his breath because the Gex launched toward him, seeming as if he was going for a strike. Clyde prepared to block it. The gex stepped to Clyde's unguarded side and was seconds away from finishing Clyde off when, luckily, a gush of water hit it right in its face knocking it off balance but not to the ground. Clyde took this chance to try and cut it down but to his surprise, the Gex was still very much aware of the situation and blocked Clyde's attack. It regained its balance and leapt back, probably to collect itself. Clyde took the opportunity to do the same. He had to hold it off for another minute at least by himself and as good as it was, Clyde was unsure of himself. Just as Clyde finished his thought, he noticed that it didn't seem focused on him but instead on Clyde's only remaining partner who was even more helpless than he was. Clyde took a reassuring breath and just as soon as the Gex made a move toward the girl, Clyde stepped in and forced the Gex's attention on him. Clyde shut his mind off and focused completely on winning this fight. He relentlessly swung his sword at the Gex, one right after the other as the Gex blocked each attack. Clyde's sword then got stuck in a chip or something on the Gex's arm leaving him wide open for the Gex to attack, or so it thought, as its attack was blocked by Clyde's kukri. The Gex took a step back and went for another slash. Clyde didn't block this one but rather dodged as the Gex slashed. Clyde barely got out of the way as the tip ripped down the eye slot of his helmet. Clyde draped his sword and got right in the Gex's face plunging his kukri deep Into its neck. The Gex, out of desperation, kicked Clyde and sent him flying about five feet back; Clyde was still able to stay on his feet with his kukri firmly in his hand. Clyde began to walk toward the Gex. The Gex began to back away from Clyde. It let out a low screech as it continued to back off. Clyde looked around to see that the other Gex were doing the same. As they slowly stepped into the safety of darkness, Clyde regrouped with the remaining people and silently waited until daybreak to arrive.

Once daybreak finally arrived, Clyde and the wounded but alive Vice-Captain made a recount of the survivors, and including Clyde, only thirteen had survived the night. Clyde approached the Vice-Captain who looked to be somewhat in shock.

"You still alive," asked Clyde, placing his hand on his shoulders.

"They got past me... they killed all of our sick and injured in mere seconds and I couldn't stop them," he said as he peered out at the bloody mess of tents.

"I know. It's not much comfort but you did everything you could possibly do and I'm sure they don't resent you," said Clyde, trying to somewhat comfort him.

"Well, I suppose we had better go back and report to the Captain before anything else happens. Would you mind being our guide, Clyde," asked the Vice-Captain almost defeatedly.

"We're going to have to be very cautious from this point onward so you had best do what you will with your dead quickly and we should be on our way," Clyde said, trying not to sound cold.

"Right... fortunately, our healer survived as well as our Little Pix, so let's try not to be too sad about it, eh fellas," said the Vice-Captain trying to improve his comrades' moods.

Pix wasn't taking the loss of so many of her comrades well, so Clyde took her place in helping bury what was left of them. The Vice-Captain seemed to understand such things as he stayed strong and quiet while digging away. As they were saying their words over the graves of their friends, Clyde began dismembering the Gex that they all had successfully killed. Surprisingly, all together they had killed four Gexes, and the Vice-Captain was able to kill two by himself which Clyde was quite impressed with. Clyde retrieved all the valuable and useful parts of the Gexes and made a makeshift sled to haul them across No Man's Land. Clyde intended to sell most of it and probably split the profit with the Vice-Captain to hopefully make up for the great loss they just had.

"Well, although things didn't turn out as ideally as I had hoped, if it wasn't for you, this many wouldn't have survived... so you have my thanks," said the Vice-Captain to Clyde before he rounded up his remaining crew.

"I suppose we should properly introduce ourselves. I'm Adauntis, Vice-Captain of the Sunset Fighters...

or what's left of them anyways," said Adauntis as he walked along side Clyde.

"You can call me Clyde, and I apologize I couldn't help much more than just warning you."

"Don't bother, you did more than you could. I shouldn't have taken the risk of coming down through here."

"Why did you all decide to come through No Man's Land," asked Clyde as he struggled a bit pushing his sled.

"Well, the boss said he was gonna be in town for another week or so to collect the payment from the caravan leader so half of us decided to begin the trip home. Well, one thing led to another and some of the boys talked me into taking this shortcut despite the nasty rumors and I guess you know the rest," said Adauntis as he helped Clyde with his sled.

"Thanks... We'll make camp right before dark. It's best not to light a fire. It's a dead giveaway of our location. Also, we'll need to take shifts and keep watch throughout the night," said Clyde, changing the subject to the present.

"Right... you hear that, boys? We're sleeping light tonight," he said, followed by a "yes sir" from his men.

The night was cold and surprisingly bright as the moon shone throughout the valley. Regardless of what Clyde said, he had trouble sleeping for a few reasons. One, his mind kept thinking that he almost ended up being one of the buried men back there and the second was that the girl they call Pix decided to sleep uncomfortably close to Clyde. *She must be cold*, Clyde thought and after a while, Clyde covered her with his bedroll as he sat beside her wrapped in his cloak.

"Why are you such a kind person," asked Pix, surprising Clyde when she was awake.

"If I'm being honest with you, I don't consider myself to be kind... I just thought of what my master would have done and acted as such."

"If that's the case, then why did you put this over me, "She asked as she rolled over and looked Clyde in the eyes as she peeked out of the blankets.

Clyde, unable to dodge her question, just decided it would be better to tease her than tell the truth.

"Because if you catch a cold, it'll be a pain to carry you all the way to town," said Clyde jokingly.

She laughed a bit before disappearing under the covers and scooted toward Clyde.

"It's truly heartbreaking to have so many of my friends disappear overnight," she said quietly underneath the blanket.

"If the world didn't throw us such challenges to overcome, then life would be too easy.... Sorry if I'm being insensitive but that just seems to be my experience so far."
"Well, insensitive as you are, you seem to have a kind heart.... Thank you," she said before falling asleep.

There was no way Clyde could find himself falling asleep with her so close to him, so he simply sat there with his cloak wrapped tightly around him as his mind was repeating the gruesome night over and over. His cloak smelled of Skye's perfume which eased Clyde's racing mind giving him pleasant memories to think about for the remainder of the long night.

It took four long days of traveling to make it to the northern port town of Rowe. Luckily, they were four long uneventful days. Once they reached the checkpoint outside the city, Adauntis paid the tax, and they entered the town with no issues.

"Well, if you'd come with us to see the Captain, I'm sure he'd like to express his gratitude," said Adauntis, hoping Clyde would go.

"Well, I've got to take care of some things I need to take care of... I am free after so I might stop by for a bit," said Clyde, knowing that he would at least come by to pay the Captain his fair share before heading home.

"W... would you mind if I came along with you," asked Pix almost half-heartedly.

"You can do what you wish," said Clyde as he began pushing the sled down the street.

"So, where all do you have to go," she asked as she casually strolled beside Clyde.

"Well, first I need to find a place to sell this stuff, then I need to find somewhere to mend my equipment.... Is there anywhere in particular you need to go while we're in the shopping district," Clyde asked trying to figure out why she tagged along.

She took a moment to answer, giving Clyde the proper chance to look at her in the daylight for once. She wore some light chainmail over a plain shirt and trousers, which although isn't very good, it's better than nothing as far as armor. Clyde couldn't help but notice that she had quite the figure even under the baggy clothes she wore.

"Umm, is there something wrong with my clothes," she asked to let Clyde know she saw him looking.

"Oh... no, I was just wondering why you wear such light chainmail with no other armor to speak of," said Clyde, attempting to dodge the bullet.

"Oh this? Well, for one, it's the best I can afford and it's also quite heavy as it is, so I don't think im ready to get a heavier set," she said as she fiddled with her chainmail.

"I see. Well, it is better than nothing that's for sure... Ahh, this is where I need to go. Do you mind watching this stuff," asked Clyde as he almost excitedly hurried to the door.

Clyde didn't wait for an answer as he walked into the shop and approached the shopkeeper.

"What can I do for you stranger," asked the curious but cautious shopkeeper.
Clyde was more than ready to try his merchant skills out that he learned from Darren but the first

big thing he had to do was make his intentions clear.

"Yes, I actually have come to sell today," said Clyde in a calm collected tone.

"Right, will you be selling for credit or perhaps cash," asked the shopkeeper.

In this situation, Clyde needs to consider a few different things: one is how often he plans on visiting this town and if he should build a relationship with these people, two is how much the shopkeeper might be willing to spend on what Clyde has, and three is how much cash is too much for a normal town shop. Considering these things, what Clyde has is worth easily forty gold neros which is a ridiculous amount of money, so Clyde was obviously going to be selling at a loss regardless.

"Have you heard of a Gex, good sir," asked Clyde.

"Of course, they're the dangerous monsters that lurk in No Man's Land."

"What would you pay for the shell and arms of such a creature?"

The shopkeeper just looked at Clyde for a moment, almost as if he were waiting for the end of some joke, until he finally answered.

"Well, I mean if you really had them, then I'd probably pay you as much as six gold neros for one if it wasn't too damaged," said the shopkeeper carefully.

Clyde thought for a moment and figured that was an agreeable price. Even though it was almost half of what it was worth, Clyde figured some credit in this town would be worth it.

"Right... I have four with me right now. Would you consider buying half on credit and half in cash," asked Clyde of the now shocked shopkeeper.

"Let me look at them before I make any final deal," said the skeptical shopkeeper.

"Of course. They're right outside."

Clyde and the shopkeeper went outside to find his sled of Gex parts still there, but his tagalong was missing. Clyde noticed that she wasn't far away and surrounded by none other than the same punks that he took care of for Dr. Montgomery a while back.

"My, my, it seems like I keep running into old friends these days," Clyde said sarcastically loud enough for the punks to hear him.

"Huh? No way. It's that guy!"

"L... let's go get us a drink guys."

"Right, it's not worth the trouble," said the punks as they briskly walked away after recognizing Clyde.

Pix seemed quite relieved to be free from the harassment and she quickly ran to Clyde's side for some reason. Clyde then turned to the shopkeeper who was entranced by the Gex parts and seemed to not even notice the commotion.

"Right, so let's hear your offer," said Clyde, getting the attention of the shopkeeper.

The older shopkeeper turned around and Clyde could now tell he was ready to do business.

"Right... what do you say to eighteen gold, half of which is credit," said the old shopkeeper without so much as a flinch in his expression.

"Hmm. I don't think so. You clearly said six for one earlier," said Clyde, trying to get the shopkeeper off balance.

"Indeed, but it seems as though these parts are quite damaged," he said trying to get Clyde to lower his price.

"Damaged and worn are two very different things. Besides, you might not ever get a chance to buy these again. Are you sure you want to pass up this big score?"

The shopkeeper broke his merchant's face for a moment before resuming the negotiations.

"Fine. I'll offer you twenty-four gold neros, half credit," said the old shopkeeper.

"Twenty-four neros and I keep this," said Clyde picking up one of the blade arms of the Gex.
The merchant stood there for a moment in thought as Clyde reached his hand out to complete the deal with the man. Reluctantly, the shopkeeper met Clyde's hand with a firm handshake and walked inside to prepare the contract.

"Well, that little bit of business is done. I'll be right back out once I get my money. Are you okay out here," asked Clyde before he walked in.

"Y... yes, of course," said Pix before Clyde entered the shop once again.
Clyde signed the contract and received his twelve gold neros, half in gold neros and half in silver neros. Afterwards he returned to Pix who was waiting patiently for him outside.

"Right then, shall we be off," asked Clyde to the patiently waiting Pix.

"Yes, of course," she said, almost as if she was startled.

She was holding the Gex arm that Clyde was planning on keeping and it seemed to be almost too much for her to carry as they began walking to their next destination.

"You know I can carry that now if you'd like. It is mine, so I should be carrying it anyway," said Clyde reaching for the arm.

"No, I'm fine. It's the least I can do," she said as she shied away from Clyde's hand.

"Very well... have you figured out what you wanted to do while we're in town?"
"Umm... yes, I'd like to get some food while we're out, if you don't mind," she said, while gripping the arm tightly.

"Sure, I could eat... would you like to do that before or after we go to the blacksmith," asked Clyde, trying to guess how hungry she might be.

"Let's go after so we have plenty of time," she said happily.

Clyde nodded and proceeded onward to the blacksmith's shop where he paid the blacksmith to allow him to use his tools and shop to do his own repairs. Clyde quickly and thoroughly repaired his weapons and armor to the best of his ability but, unfortunately, the gash in his helmet was unfixable so he would have to make do with it until he got home to make a new one. Clyde even took the time to perform maintenance on Pix's gear while he was at it and explained to her some different options for armor and weapons she should try when she had the money. Soon after they were finished and wandering about the streets.

"So, would you like to eat at a street stall or find us an inn or tavern to eat at," asked Clyde as he was stretching his now tired arms.

"L... let's find us an inn," she said almost as if she was unsure.

"Alrighty. Sounds good. Do you know any good ones around these parts?"

"Yes, there's one by the docks that's quite nice," she said as she took the lead as Clyde followed behind.

Once they got to the inn, Clyde couldn't help but notice how busy the place was. There were sailors and fisherman as well as just day drinkers from the looks of things. Clyde followed Pix to the counter as he listened to her talk to the barkeep.

"Y... yes, we would like to sit and eat please," she said as loud as she seemed to be able to talk so the man could hear her over the commotion.

"Sorry lass, all the tables are full... We do have some empty rooms you could rent for the night... We could bring your dinner up to you there," said the barkeep as he glanced back to Clyde then back to her.

"We'll take it," she said quickly.

Clyde couldn't help but notice that her hands were shaking as she took the room key from the barkeep. Something was going on, but Clyde couldn't quite put his finger on what she was trying to pull. Clyde watched her carefully as she led the way to the room and struggled to open the door with the key. She sat quietly as Clyde set his weapons and pack down and they both waited patiently for the food to arrive. Clyde ate his meal but kept watching Pix as she barely ate any of her food but rather seemed as thou she was thinking something over and it was bothering her a great deal. Clyde stopped eating and cleaned his mouth before looking her in the eye.

"Alright, let's hear what's on your mind before you worry yourself to death," said Clyde right before he took a drink of the strong ale she ordered.

"Well... I want to repay you for helping us and saving my life when those monsters attacked... but I don't have any money or anything so I figured once we were here, I'd be able to pay you back the only way I can," she said as she couldn't look at Clyde and her face turned red.

After a moment, Clyde realized what she had planned to do, and it left him quite speechless. For a moment, all he could do was look at her.

"Uhh, um, wait just a minute here," Clyde finally said as he was trying to race through his mind for a solution.

Pix took a deep breath and got up from her seat and approached the nervous Clyde. Clyde then snapped out of his trance and jumped out of his seat, laying his hands on Pix's shoulder stopping her.

"Listen... I truly appreciate that you feel this strongly about repaying me but... you don't have to go this far for something like that," explained Clyde, trying to de-escalate the situation.

"How else can I repay you for putting your life on the line to save people that have done nothing but hurt you," she asked as tears began to form in her eyes.

As much as Clyde wanted to just go along with her, he couldn't help but notice that she was pushing herself into doing it. He could smell the alcohol on her breath as well as feel her trembling as he was holding her shoulders. No matter what way he looked at it, the right thing to do was reject her but he was trying to think of a way to do it that would avoid tears.

"Listen... we don't know hardly anything about one another. The only thing I know about you is that, despite your actions, you tried to make amends for them, and I can only respect that. Also, you saved my life first if you remember during all that mess. And lastly, you can't thank me because I couldn't even save half of your comrades back there so as far as I see it were even," explained Clyde carefully, hoping that was sufficient.

Unfortunately for Clyde, it didn't stop the tears because right after Clyde let go, she wrapped herself around him and began crying despite his efforts. The only thing he could do was try to comfort her and deal with it. She cried for a good twenty minutes mentioning some names of supposedly the friends she lost and mumbling some other alcohol-induced things before she finally fell asleep. Clyde then laid her down in the bed and covered her up and locked the door before leaving so no one could bother her. Clyde sighed a deep sigh before going downstairs to the main floor where a familiar face was waiting for him.

"Well, I would say it looks like you had a good night, but you look more stressed than I do," said the man inviting Clyde over to sit.

"So, you're the Captain of these guys," asked Clyde to confirm his suspicion.

"I guess I had better properly introduce myself. The name is Luther Hildebrand. I'm glad we're meeting on somewhat better terms this time," he said as he extended his hand out to Clyde.

"Clyde Galkerson. It's a pleasure," said Clyde as he accepted the man's handshake.

"So, just to keep things sincere, our Little Pix didn't get carried away did she," Luther asked almost threateningly.

"No, she just drank a bit too much and fell asleep," Clyde carefully responded.

"Good... so if I remember correctly, you're the fellow that earned my respect in the last town, correct? Judging by the fact that you caught up with us so quickly means that you actually went through No Man's Land, yes," asked Luther curiously.

"Well, yes... it's actually my second full trip to this town going that way," replied Clyde after he ordered some cheap grog from the barkeep.
"Second? My, my, that's impressive. Did you have similar trouble the first time?"

"Not necessarily, although I've observed the Gex. I've only ever killed one other in my experience traversing the area," explained Clyde, leaving out the fact that the first one was definitely easier to deal with.

"Well, that must be quite the tale!... But unfortunately, I don't quite have the time to hear it out. So on to business then. I believe I owe you some compensation for your help from what I've been told," he said as he reached in his jacket.

"No, no, I'm the one that owes you," said Clyde, stopping him from continuing.

"Oh, what makes you say that?"

"I've accepted part of what the Gex parts were worth as compensation and as for the rest, I'm giving it to you to hopefully build your guild back," said Clyde, producing a pouch with ten gold neros worth of coin.
"You do realize just how much money this is, right," said Luther as he looked at the contents of the pouch.

"Carrying all that home would be quite a hassle anyway so don't worry about it," said Clyde, blowing the question off.

"Well, if you're heading back south, let me propose a different way to pay you back then," said Luther as he put the pouch securely in his jacket.

Clyde's curiosity was peaked as he had no idea what kind of offer he was going to make.

"Listen, my contact has asked me if I knew anyone who could navigate the shortcut through No Man's Land because he had a wealthy client who needed passage and was in dire need to get through. If you're interested, I could arrange a talk. The decision to accept will be between you and the client," said Luther right before he took a long drink of ale.

Clyde pondered for a moment deciding whether or not he should try and get another person or group through No Man's Land or not.

"I'll talk to the client and see where it goes from there," said Clyde finally.

"Great, I'll send someone in the morning to introduce you," Luther said with a smile as he got up and walked out of the inn.

Clyde then asked the barkeep over and rented the room next to the one Pix was in and he tried his best to sleep.

Chapter 6: Big Jobs

Despite Clyde's mostly calm demeanor throughout the past few days, he was quite distressed on the inside. He kept wondering what he could have done to stop so many of them from getting killed. He couldn't help but wonder if he could have worked better with the ones in his group, they wouldn't have died. The sounds of the confusing night kept creeping up in Clyde's mind throughout the quiet night. Clyde finally drifted off to sleep for a few hours before he woke to a soft knocking on his door.

"Yes," Clyde said softly as he slowly opened the door.

Pix was standing in the hallway, her face was noticeably red, as she obviously wouldn't make eye contact with Clyde.

"Y... you're not wearing your armor, I see," she said nervously.

Clyde didn't know what to say to her obvious observation, so he simply stayed quiet and waited for her to gather her thoughts.

"The Commander sent me to.... to bring you to the meeting... or something," she said, finally getting to the point.

"Right. Give me a bit and let me put my armor on," Clyde said as he attempted to close the door back.

"U... um..." Pix said, quickly making Clyde pause to see what else she wanted.

"Yes?"

"It would be much faster if I assisted you... perhaps as an apology for my... unruly behavior last night," she said, getting quieter as she spoke.

Clyde was frankly too tired to argue with her, so he humored her as he motioned her in. She happily followed behind Clyde, closing the door quietly behind her. Although Clyde had accepted her help, he wasn't very comfortable with having someone watch, let alone help him put his armor on. To Clyde's surprise, as he sat down after putting his leather lined trousers on, she was waiting for him to let her put his breastplate on. She seemed quite adept at what she was doing as she tightened the laces on each piece of Clyde's armor snugly and quickly. Clyde had designed his armor to be easier for one person to put on, but he couldn't help but enjoy the help he was getting. Once she had finished lacing Clyde's boots, he was ready to go in less than half the time he would have been if he had done it himself and he noticed that his armor felt as if it fit better as well.

"Well, I must say, that was nicer than I thought it would be... thank you," said Clyde as he was testing the fit on his armor.

Pix seemed to enjoy Clyde's praise as she walked to the door.

"Right, hurry along, I'll be waiting downstairs," she said, seeming to gain her confidence back.

"I'm surprised how nice she is after what I almost did last night," said Clyde to himself hoping that she doesn't think he was trying to take advantage of her.

"I suppose I'd better not make her wait," he said as he quickly threw his weapons on and locked the door as he left.

As Clyde walked down the stairs of the inn, which seemed to serve more as a brothel, he saw Pix waiting for him. She seemed almost unable to stay still as she stood there fidgeting with her hands and feet. Clyde assumed she felt uncomfortable being around him after what happened last night.

"I'll be back later tonight. Do you need me to pay now or later for another night," Clyde asked the innkeeper.

"You can pay before you leave. I know you're good for it," he said as he shooed Clyde on to get them out of the inn, probably so he could take a break from his inn responsibilities.

"Apologies for keeping you waiting," Clyde said, breaking Pix out of her impatient position.

"R... right, let's go," she said as she jumped toward the door.

Clyde followed along obediently as she walked fast through the busy morning streets near the port of the town. Clyde couldn't help but notice he was having trouble keeping up with Pix's quick pace as she effortlessly weaved through the crowds. She finally decided to stop outside of a building seemingly to wait for Clyde to catch up. And once he had, she began to speak to him.

"About last night... wh... why did you turn me down? Is it because I'm not attractive or mature enough for you," she asked, seemingly out of nowhere, catching Clyde off guard.
"What?! Where did that come from," asked Clyde, trying to avoid answering that trap of a question.

"Well... you turned me down last night and I just want to know what you don't see in me," she said, still avoiding eye contact with Clyde.

"Listen Pix, there's nothing about you that I find unappealing, and the fact that you even think like that proves how mature you are... How about this? After I meet with this guy, I'll take you out on the town and we'll have a good time as a way of me apologizing," Clyde said, hoping to at least make her feel better about herself.

"You promise," she said almost childlike.

"I promise."

Pix continued to lead the way into the building followed closely by Clyde. They didn't even stop at the counter. Instead, they went straight up the stairs to a private room that was obviously used to hold meetings and the like. Pix stepped to the side and directed Clyde to go inside. Clyde hesitantly opened the door to find Luther sitting down and drinking what seemed to be some kind of alcohol.

"Well, hello there, Clyde. I'm glad you found your way so quickly!! Unfortunately, though, our other party is running behind so you can just relax here. I'll be sure to direct him in once he arrives," he said, almost jumping out of the room and closing the door behind him, leaving Clyde all alone.

"Wonder what all that's about," Clyde said to himself quietly.

Clyde sat in the room and waited patiently. After what seemed to be an hour, Clyde heard Luther's voice outside the room.

"Yes sir, he's been waiting patiently for your arrival," he said, right as the door flung open.

Who stood in the doorway was obviously a well-off man simply by looking at his clothing as well as his facial expression. The man was somewhat shorter than Clyde himself but stood taller than anyone Clyde had met. His clothes were noticeably expensive and well-made despite the fact that they weren't exactly flashy. The man had trimmed dark hair and a light tan presumably from his recent travels. What followed this man into the room was not far from monsters. They stood easily a foot taller than Clyde and the pure muscle on them was visible through their cheap gambesons. They were more than likely his bodyguards which made Clyde wonder why he was even considered to escort him across No Man's Land in the first place.

"Ahh, so you must be Clyde! How wonderful to meet you," said the man surprisingly enthusiastically.

"Likewise, Sir. Um, excuse me but I'm afraid I don't have the pleasure of knowing your name," Clyde replied as formally as possible.

The man seemed to be somewhat surprised for a moment that Clyde showed manners. He quickly recovered and replied. "Oh well, of course, you may address me as Lord Jaren Travitson, owner and founder of the Pristine Jade Company. Since I've taken a liking to you, we can speak informally with the name Jaren," he said proudly with somewhat of a laugh at the end.

"I appreciate that you think we can speak informally in such a short time, Lord Jaren," Clyde said, attempting to keep things respectful.

"Well, I'm a good judge of character and I can already tell that you're going to be worth investing in. So, let's get down to the business at hand," said Jaren as he sat down across from Clyde.

As soon as he sat down, his aura changed to a noticeably serious one making Clyde feel somewhat uneasy.

"Well, about that," Clyde said before getting cut off.

"You don't want to take the job because you're not confident in your skills. Is that about right," Jaren said without any remorse. "Since that's the case, why don't you tell me how much it would cost to change my mind," he continued with a grin.

Clyde thought for a moment and decided to throw out a ridiculous price that would make Jaren back down.

"Sixty gold is my price," Clyde said plainly to the unflinching Jaren.

Jaren thought for a moment then leaned back almost as if he was relieved. He thought for a moment and seemed to come to a conclusion as he looked Clyde firmly in the eyes.

"Well then, you'll be paid one hundred and twenty gold: half now and half upon completion. I'll see you in the morning," he said confidently as he stood up.

"W...wait. There's one more thing," Clyde said, stopping Jaren before he could leave... "I have three rules that you must agree to follow first."

"Well, let's hear these rules of yours," Jarren said, fully addressing Clyde.

"Firstly, you must follow any order I give. Secondly, never go on your own. And lastly, you're not allowed to die," Clyde said, waiting for a response.

Jaren stepped closer to Clyde and slapped him on the shoulder with a laugh.

"You see, I told you I was going to like you. I agree with your rules, and I will see you at sunrise in the morning," he said before exiting, leaving in Clyde's hands a bag full of gold.

"W...wait!! Why are you offering me so much," asked Clyde, trying to find some reason to turn his offer down.

Jaren looked back and smiled at Clyde again before answering.

"Listen... I'm a good judge of character and I know who I do and don't want to do business with. And saying that, the reason I am paying you so much is simply considered an investment because for one, I have another job I wish for you to do if you impress me enough and, also, I have a feeling that we will be good friends in the future. So please just accept my generosity and leave it at that Clyde." At his answer, Clyde could only nod at him before he left.

Clyde waited a while before leaving the room as he tried to process what he had just agreed to.

"So essentially he's paying me a ridiculous amount of money to escort him across No Man's Land. The thing I've got to figure out is why. Does he want to try and hire me permanently or is he some sort of crime boss or something keeping me well paid, so I don't talk. I had best try to look into him a bit before tomorrow and see if anyone knows who he is."

After finally getting his thoughts together, he finally stood up and exited the room. As he made his way out of the building, he found Pix patiently waiting for him outside.

"How did it go? Did he actually hire you," Pix curiously asked.

"Well, he apparently liked me enough to offer an irresistible amount of money. Say, do you know anything about him," Clyde asked as they began walking together.

"Well, of course I know about him. He's one of the wealthiest men in the kingdom. I've never actually spoken to him though. What was he like?"

"Well, he was a lot nicer than he looks. How did he end up so wealthy? Is there a story behind it or did he just inherit his wealth," Clyde asked as they stopped at a vacant side street.

"Well, the rumor is that he used to be a slave and once his master died, he took over his business as a slave trader and within just ten years, he's the third largest slave trader on the continent."

"Interesting. I was unaware how large slave trading was," said Clyde, feeling a bit uneasy being hired by a slave trader.

"Well, in this area, not many folks have enough money to own slaves but not too far north or east of here close to the capital or one of the cities, it's quite common to have slaves," Pix said as she began walking again.

"Well, I'm sick of talking about business. How about I pay up on my promise? Is there anywhere you would like to go, Pix," Clyde asked, dropping the subject.

"Yes, I've actually got somewhere in mind. There's a wonderful market by the docks with some bizarre food stalls. I've always wanted to try but the leader always told me not to waste my money on them. Could we please go there," Pix asked excitedly, almost childlike.

"Well, let me run by a shop first to get my supplies ready for tomorrow and if I have enough money, we'll go check out this dock of yours," Clyde said, only to get her to worry a bit knowing full well he had plenty of cash to buy her whatever she wanted.

"Oh… are you leaving tomorrow?... If you don't have the money, I'm fine with simply going to the docks to look at all the big boats," Pix said, trying to be considerate.

"Hee, hee, alright then. Let's get a move on," Clyde said, taking the lead to the shop he sold the Gex parts at.

"Welcome. What can I do for you today," asked the shopkeeper once he saw Clyde and Pix enter the store.

"Well, I'm heading out in the morning. I was hoping I could get some supplies with the credit I have with you," Clyde said.

The shopkeeper finished what he was doing and dusted his apron off before facing Clyde.

"What supplies do you need," he asked, pulling a piece of charcoal and walking over to the counter which had some parchment on it.

"I'll need seven days' worth of rations that doesn't need to be cooked and maybe you could find a bit of armor that would fit the lady here," said Clyde, surprising Pix.

"Wait, you don't have to do that," said Pix, tugging on Clyde's sleeve.

"I don't have to but I'm going to. Once you get some decent armor, so long as you take care of it, you'll have a much better chance at surviving. This evening is my treat as a farewell," said Clyde, not giving Pix any room to talk him out of it.

After Pix quit fussing about not needing armor, the shopkeeper got what Clyde had requested and with a few extra bits Clyde used to fit Pix's armor and making some adjustments for her, it still only came out to two gold neros worth of his credit which only made Clyde feel a bit bad for the shopkeeper for giving him so much cash. Although Pix's armor was expensive, she seemed a bit embarrassed letting Clyde make adjustments while she was wearing the armor. After she walked around in it for a bit, Clyde could definitely tell she already loved it, which made him feel pretty good about giving her a useful present.

"I'll stop by in the morning to pick up the rations and all," said Clyde to the shopkeeper before leaving with Pix.

"Now, don't forget to wear your chainmail under your armor. It might be heavy at first, but you'll get used to it," Clyde said to the half listening Pix as they walked toward the docks.

The closer they got to the market at the docks, the busier the streets became with people trading and peddling all sorts of things from fish to cloth to odd trinkets from far away. It was well after midday as Clyde noticed they were already lighting the streetlamps and some of the shops seemed to be preparing to close up shop for the day. The street stalls seemed to only be getting started as the smell of freshly cooked food radiated through the area carried by the salty cool sea breeze. Clyde only thought for a second that winter was well on its way when his hand suddenly became warm and when he looked, he realized that Pix had taken the lead and was trying to get Clyde to move faster through the crowd. He couldn't help but to find himself enjoying his evening.

Clyde and Pix went to almost every stall that was open trying food, drinks, and listening to stories from all kinds of different places. At the end of the evening, Pix could hardly stand whether it was from overeating or from all the free drinks she was swindling from the people running the stalls. Clyde ended up having to carry her piggyback back to the inn. On his way back, he noticed that he wasn't fully steady himself, probably from a combination of drinks and the small girl on his back throwing off his balance. Clyde was successful making his way back through the dimly lit street when he accidentally bumped into someone. In order to keep his passenger on his back, Clyde had to drop to one knee to steady himself before he looked up preparing to apologize.

"Ahh... my apologies. I wasn't paying attention to where I was going," Clyde said, trying to get a good look at the person he bumped into. He couldn't hardly see him as one of the streetlights was burning bright directly behind the man's head obscuring Clyde's vision.

"You had best be more care.... Wait a minute. I've seen you before," said the man with a familiar voice.

"You're that guy that caused some trouble a while back. What are you doing with that poor girl?

Maybe my guys were right about you last time," said the man, getting quite angry after recognizing Clyde.

"Excuse me? I believe you've got the wrong idea," said Clyde, realizing that he's talking to the same guy that almost fought him during his last visit in this town.

"A man carrying a young woman that's too drunk to know where she's at in the middle of the night to somewhere she shouldn't be... Yea, I've got a feeling I know what's going on and I warned you last time about stirring up trouble," said the man as he took a step closer to Clyde.

"I don't know where you got that Idea from but I assure you I'm simply taking her back to the inn so she can sleep off the alcohol," said Clyde, standing back up with Pix still on his back.

"Hate to be a jerk but I simply don't trust you at all, so I'm gonna ask nicely for you to hand her over to me so I can make sure she's gonna be fine," said the man. Clyde could feel his aura almost as if an ocean breeze was coming from him.

"I'm afraid that trust thing goes both ways. If you're so worried about her, I don't mind you tagging along, buy you will not be taking her from me without resistance," said Clyde, hoping he takes the less aggressive option.

Surprisingly, his presence and body language softened as he thought it over.

"Alright. I'm in no hurry right now. Let's go to this inn," he said as he gestured for Clyde to lead the way.

As they walked along quietly, Clyde could only think that they couldn't get to the inn quick enough until the man spoke up again.

"So, how long have you been a mercenary," asked the man with a serious expression.

"Well, to be completely honest, I wouldn't really call myself a mercenary. I've just done some work for people who've asked," Clyde said with a forced smile.

"I see... so what was your last job all about with that drunk," said the man.

Clyde could tell he was obviously trying to gauge what kinda person he was so Clyde thought it would be best to answer instead of avoiding the conversation.

"Well, that drunk was actually a doctor and this little girl in the village south of here was in some serious trouble unless someone went and got him, so I went and got him."

The look of surprise blew over the man's face as if he didn't believe a word of what Clyde said. (This man couldn't lie to save his life.) Clyde thought to himself.

"Well, what brings you here this time," he asked almost immediately after Clyde's thought.

"Well, this time is more of a coincidence, I was in No Man's Land hunting Gex when I stumbled across this girl and her group trying to take a shortcut to this town. I decided to go and warn them about the Gex, then they ended up under attack by the beasts. I got stuck helping the ones that survived here."

"And why are you carrying her to an inn," he asked persistently.

"Well, I landed a good paying escort job heading south in the morning and apparently she took a liking to me, so I figured I'd let her have some fun eating and drinking my coin purse away as a farewell," Clyde said, almost hating his own words.

The man's face twisted into concern and confusion as he seemed to digest his answered questions as they walked and soon the inn finally came within site.

"Well, this is our stop. Would you like to come in for a drink," asked Clyde being polite.

"No, I believe this is far enough for me... I didn't ever catch your name."

"Clyde Galkerston and yourself?"

"You can call me Rye," he said gently and confidently.

"Like the bread," Clyde asked without much thought.

"That's right! My fa... I mean, my master gave me that name when he caught me stealing rye bread from him as an orphan. After a sound scolding, he fed me and took me under his wing until I inherited this guild," Rye said proudly.

"Well Rye, it was a pleasure to get the water under the bridge between us. You're an interesting fellow to talk to," Clyde said, extending his hand while trying to support Pix with his other one.

"The feeling is mutual. It's nice to talk to someone that isn't trying to pull the wool over your eyes. Next time I see you, I'll make sure to take the time to grab that drink," he said as he grabbed Clyde's hand, shaking it firmly.

Clyde carried Pix into the inn and asked the innkeeper to let him into her room to put her to bed. The innkeeper, without question, grabbed the key and led the way to her room. Clyde laid the barely conscious Pix down gently on her bed and removed her boots before pulling the blanket over her and leaving. Clyde thanked the innkeeper with a few copper coins and went on to his room. Upon opening his door, he was greeted by none other than Luther reading a book in the candlelight.

"Oh, welcome back, I didn't expect you to be out so late," Luther said, closing his book.

"And what business did you have with me," asked Clyde, a bit annoyed at how easily the innkeeper let people into rooms.

"Well, I simply wanted to talk to you before you departed in the morning and this was the only place I knew you would eventually be, so I waited here."

"What did you want to talk about," asked Clyde as he began packing his things for tomorrow.

"Well, I've come to ask if you'd like to take Pix with you. You're the first person outside of the guild she's really taken a liking to and to be honest with you, our guild isn't leading her down the right path... We're a low tier merc guild which means that, basically, we not only get the scummy jobs, but we also can't afford to turn away guild members even if they have a rough history. I've known the girl all her life and our guild is just big enough now that I can't always keep an eye out for her. This last incident proved that and if you weren't there, she would have been killed. So how about it," he asked.

Clyde could tell that he didn't want to let Pix go and that he wasn't just bluffing about his feelings. Silence loomed over the room as Clyde stood still in thought.

"Well sir, as much as I would enjoy her company, I'm afraid I'll have to decline. In all honesty, what happened in No Man's Land was simply luck that the few of us that survived did," Clyde said, sitting down on the bed.

"From what I've been told, you're stronger than you say, my boy. What's the problem with having a mage watch your back?"

"Because without magic, I can't guarantee anyone's safety, that's why I dislike taking escort jobs. What's stopping you from being able to watch over Pix anyway. It's not like she has to be on the combat side of your guild," said Clyde, beginning to get frustrated at not only this uncomfortable conversation but the lack of his abilities.

"What do you mean," Luther said with a puzzled look.

"Let her handle the guild's paperwork and money. It's not only a safe position but it's important enough that she won't feel discarded," said Clyde as Luther's face went into a frustrated thought.

"She doesn't know how to read and by no means can she afford to learn."

"How much does it cost," Clyde asked almost demandingly.

"Well, when I learned, it cost around fifteen gold neros. It's hard to say how much it is now."
"Meet me at the shop close to the southern gate. I'll set some lessons up for Pix if I can afford it," Clyde said as he resumed packing his things.

"You mean you're going to pay for her lessons," asked Luther, seemingly confused.

"I should have enough credit and cash left to afford the bulk of the price. That way we both know that she's taken care of for a while, and if by chance she wants to continue jobs then she could come learn a bit about No Man's Land with me. After she learns how to read and how to manage money properly, she can make her own decisions," Clyde said as he began cleaning and sharpening his sword.

"That sounds better than sending her off with a stranger... Thank you for helping me help her. I never thought of having someone else manage the bookwork of the guild."

"I'm glad I could help clear your mind... It is quite late, so I'm going to turn in, if you don't mind," Clyde said, gesturing toward the door.

"Right, I'll leave you to it then. I'll see you in the morning," Luther said as he left.

Clyde finished his preparations and tried to sleep. He lay awake most of the night regretting that he hadn't taken Luther's offer to have Pix join him. Clyde finally drifted off to sleep after convincing himself that he made the right decision. Clyde woke up just as the sun began to slip through the window. After strapping his weapons and pack on, he left the inn behind him as he made his way to the shop.

"Well, you're quite early, aren't ya," the shopkeeper said as he was getting the sleep out of his eyes.

"Well, as you know, time is money," Clyde said, wondering what the old shopkeeper would say.
He simply flashed a smile as he put the sack of supplies Clyde had requested on the counter.

"There ya go. Luckily, I had everything you need in stock so there's no delivery charge to you," said the old man, writing in his ledger book.

"Is there anything else I can do for you," the shopkeeper asked after he noticed Clyde was still there.

Clyde had intended to wait for Luther, but after a few minutes, he realized his new client was probably waiting at the gate, so he decided to ask ahead.

"Well actually, about the rest of my credit."

"Surely you don't want to cash out at this time of day," the old man said almost irritated.

"No, nothing like that. I was wondering if you would clear my credit in exchange for a favor." At

Clyde's statement, the old man put his business face on as if he were about to lose money.

"What kind of favor," asked the old shopkeeper.

"Do you recall the young girl I bought armor for yesterday?"

The shopkeeper nodded in response.

"Well, I was wondering if you could teach her to read, write, and manage money," Clyde asked. He didn't get an immediate response from the old man who seemed to be mulling it over.

"You want me to take her as my apprentice," the old man finally said.

"More or less I suppose. Her guild leader wishes for her to help manage the business of the guild and I figured you would be a swell teacher," Clyde said, hoping to butter him up a bit.

"Well, I suppose that wouldn't be a problem. I don't plan on telling her you paid for it though. I'm going to make her earn her keep instead. It makes them learn faster when they think they're earning it themselves," said the old man with a smile.

"Very well could you write out a contract then," Clyde asked quickly.

"What? Don't you trust the word of a merchant? Whoever taught you knows their stuff," the old man said, almost laughing.

Once the contract was drawn up, Clyde signed as well as the old man just as Luther walked in the door.

"Right, here you go," said Clyde as he handed Luther the contract.

"What's this now," he asked as he began to read it. "This man will be her teacher. You can hash the details out later. I'm running late so I need to go." Clyde took off before Luther could ask any more questions.

Clyde made his way to the town gate where his client was waiting patiently with his two bodyguards.

Chapter 7: The Slaver

Once Clyde came within sight of Jaren, he began waving at Clyde.

"Well, well, look who's finally showing up. Did you have a long night," asked Jaren with a suspicious tone.

"I had some last-minute business to take care of. My apologies," Clyde said bowing his head.

"We're still ahead of schedule. No worries on my end. Are you ready to go now," Jaren asked.

"Well, if you don't mind, I actually have some things I wish to ask you first."

Jaren made an almost exhausted expression after Clyde said as much.

"I suppose you've found out who I am and you're wondering if I should help a large slave trader on his journey to possibly buy more slaves. Is that it," asked Jaren, seemingly annoyed.

"Almost," Clyde said, causing Jaren to noticeably take notice.

"I've heard that you've lived an interesting life and to end up where you are is quite odd to me, so I was wondering..."

"You were wondering why a former slave could possibly become a slaver. Is that it," interrupted Jaren.

Clyde only nodded his head.

"How about this? Why don't you let me tell you along the way and if you don't like it, you're free to abandon us or whatever you feel like doing. Is that satisfactory," asked Jaren.

"Sounds like you have too much faith in me, but I suppose we're losing daylight," Clyde said as he took the lead and began walking.

They walked silently until they actually left the main road and started down into No Man's Land when Jaren finally began his story.

"The earliest memories I have are of when I got my brand and when the master was teaching me how to read: both of which were full of pain and punishments. Once I came of age, the master took me under his wing and taught me how to manage his finances and pretty much do his job for him," Jaren said as he was sifting through his memories.

Clyde only listened carefully as he made his way to and then over the ravine. He noticed that although Jaren seemed quite the nobility, he didn't have any trouble traversing the rugged landscape as he walked and talked.

"I worked like that for almost twenty years when the master came to me one day and told me something I never imagined he would say."

"What did he tell you," asked Clyde curiously.

"Well, he said he was going to die tomorrow, and I was the only one he trusted leaving his company to so get ready to own it or sell it, boy," Jaren said as he stopped walking.

"Surprisingly enough, he had the paperwork all set up and although his children and wife tried everything they could, I ended up with a mediocre slave trading company within a week of him telling me that," said Jaren, half laughing at his memory.

Clyde didn't want to believe such a wild story, but Jaren didn't seem to be lying as far as Clyde could tell.

"Why didn't you just sell it and be free," asked Clyde.

"Well, I have two reasons: firstly, slave trading was all I knew how to do and secondly, it would never fix the problem that slavery is," Jaren said quite seriously.

Clyde could only look at him confused until he continued his explanation.

"Listen my boy, people have been doing this whole slavery thing wrong and I'm trying to do it the way it should be done. I go to auctions and sales and buy all the weak, unwanted, or troublesome slaves, then I send them to get cleaned and fed at my nearest facility. I then ask them what job they either have an interest in or is already proficient in and train them to be good at that job. I also teach all the ones interested how to read and write. Then I only sell to customers that have positive histories with slaves to give them the best life possible. And since they're worth so much more, they're very unlikely to be mistreated, in case I don't know the customer," explained Jaren extensively.

Although Clyde could only take him at his word, he felt that Jaren was in fact telling him nothing but the truth.

"Well, at the very least, you're one convincing fellow," said Clyde as he began to keep walking.

"M... master Jaren has always done us right," said the larger of the two bodyguards.

"He bought us before we were sent to our deaths in the arena for killing our previous master," said the smaller of the two.

"Well, these two took a lot of work to get the whole kill whatever was in the same room out of them," said Jaren.

"By the way, the larger one is Tug and the smaller is Drue. Apologies for not introducing them properly," Jaren said as he was struggling to climb a steep hill.

"So, are you both slaves," asked Clyde as he lent a hand to Drue after he reached the top.

"Yes, we are the master's personal travel slaves," said Tug as he helped his brother.

"Do you enjoy being slaves," Clyde asked as he helped Jaren.

"Master doesn't make us fight unless we choose to so long as we protect him when the time comes. So, he is much better than our last master who made us kill in the arena," said Tug once they began walking again.

"And master does not starve us even if we make a mistake," Drue said as he was following Tug.

"Then what's the point of having slave crests on them," Clyde asked Jaren.

"Well, there's a few reasons actually: firstly, if one happens to go missing for some reason, I can use it to track their location ;secondly, if they for some reason get out of control, I can use it to bring them back to their senses; and lastly, it proves that they belong somewhere so any legal issues come straight to me," said Jaren as he begins to look tired.

Clyde looked to the sky to judge the time. He noticed they had possibly three hours before nightfall and decided this would be a good enough place to set up for the night.

"Let's call it a day. We'll set up camp here," Clyde said as he dropped his bag.

Clyde was rolling out his bedroll when he noticed that Tug and Drue were starting a fire.

"Hey!! Don't start a fire," Clyde barked as he kicked dirt over their embers.

"How are we going to stay warm," asked Drue

"And what about dinner," asked Tug.

"A fire will attract some unwanted attention from the dangerous wildlife so you're going to have to eat things that don't need to be cooked, and as far as warmth, you'll just have to deal with it," Clyde said quite seriously.

"But almost all of our food needs to be cooked," Tug said almost sadly.

"Let me make the fire... Then we'll look at what you have to cook," Clyde said, almost feeling bad for snapping at them.

Clyde began to dig two narrow holes about three feet apart from each other and almost a foot deep. He then connected the two with a hole underground before gathering his kindling for the fire.

"What is it that you're doing," asked Jaren as he watched Clyde closely.

"Well, this is what you call a Dakoda fire hole. My father taught me how to make it," Clyde said as he was blowing the freshly lit kindling.

"What's so special about it," asked Jaren.

"Well, for one, it reduces the smoke quite a bit and it being buried in the ground makes it difficult to see from a distance," explained Clyde.

"Here is our food. We have dried meat and potatoes," said Drue, handing Clyde the metal pot with the food inside.

Clyde questioningly looked at Drue and Tug as they seemed quite excited to eat. Clyde shrugged and got some water and pepper out of his bag as well as a piece of salted meat he prepared a while back. He then poured the water into the pot and placed it into the hole where the fire was. Once the potatoes were cooked, he cut up the meat and sprinkled some of the pepper into the pot letting it simmer for a bit to loosen the tough meat. Once the meat and potatoes were cooked how Clyde liked it, he took the pot off the fire and prepared four bowls full and he added a few herbs he had gathered while they were walking which Skye used quite frequently to make stew boiled in water taste almost like it was boiled in proper broth. After Clyde handed out the bowls of stew, he covered the fire with dirt to smother it out quickly.

"My, my, this is quite impressive. I've never had food quite this tasty whilst traveling," Jaren said as he was hastily eating his stew.

Drue and Tug seemed too busy eating to be able to speak which made Clyde feel as though he satisfied their want for a good meal. Once the sun began to set, the temperature began to drop with it. And soon after, it began to snow. The four huddled together for warmth from the elements as Clyde took the first watch. Although it was snowing quite heavily, surprisingly Clyde could still see as the bright moon peeked through the cloudy sky. The moon was only half full, yet it was incredibly bright. Clyde decided to just stay awake throughout the quiet night, not out of any sympathy toward his heavily sleeping companions but because it was quite simply nice to enjoy a calm peaceful night. *Winter has fully set in,* Clyde thought to himself as he held himself tightly under his cloak warm with memories.

"Alright. It's time to get a move on," Clyde said as he shook the others awake just before daybreak.

"You stayed awake all night," asked Jaren as he rubbed the sleep from his eyes.

"It was a calm night so I figured I'd let you all rest while you can," said Clyde as he gathered the empty pot and settled it in his bag.

The group set off again through the, now, snow-covered No Man's Land. Clyde could just barely recognize the landmarks as it seemed the snow had completely changed everything. The snow made the journey almost twice as difficult as slopes were slick and holes hidden by snow. They made camp a bit earlier than the first day hoping to regain some energy. Clyde cooked for the group again which made Drue and Tug quite happy. They both insisted that Clyde actually sleep and that they would keep watch which although Clyde tried to fight it, he reluctantly went to sleep.

"Wake up. It's snowed again," said Tug as he shook Clyde awake.

"I guess we had better get moving then," Clyde said as he stretched himself awake.

The snow was almost a foot deep and the tracks they had made yesterday were long covered up. Clyde found it odd that it only seemed to snow at night when during the day the sky was as clear as can be. Regardless, the cold was not going anywhere. It seemed as his fingers felt as though they would fall off if he wasn't wearing gloves. The next three days was just as uneventful except that the snow had stopped. On the fourth day, they had made it to the valley which Clyde normally climbed up the side and traveled along the plateau.

"Seems as though we had better travel along the lower road. Climbing up there seems like a deathtrap to me," said Jaren as he sat down to catch his breath.

"Well, as much as I hate changing the route, it seems like the best option," said Clyde as he began down into the valley.

After about midday, they were about a fourth through the valley. There didn't seem to be any sign of other life anywhere around which only worried Clyde as they continued along. Clyde was out front leading the way when he stepped on something that made an odd noise. Fear instantly took over Clyde's senses as he instinctively reached for his sword. He didn't even have time to draw it because what he had stepped on was a sleeping Gex covered in snow. It jolted awake and it's bladed arm was inches away from Clyde's throat. The next thing Clyde knew was he was jerked backwards just in time for the Gex to miss its mark. Drue was the one who yanked Clyde back, sending him falling back. Once Clyde struggled back to his feet, he looked to see Tug and Drue standing off with the Gex.

"Be careful. They are better fighters than you think. They're also normally in a group so we need to watch for more," said Clyde as he took a few steps toward them.

"Don't you worry. We can handle this fight. You just stay safe so you can cook us something good tonight," said Tug as he took a step toward the Gex.

At that moment, the Gex began to lunge toward Tug as quickly as ever. Tug smacked its blade off course, then almost in the same motion he punched it right in the head, crushing it instantly. The Gex fell to the ground twitching as the life left its body. Clyde was almost in shock that he did that with only his fist, but he didn't have time to admire him as three more Gex burst up from the snow: two of which were going for Tug and Drue and the last seemed to be aiming for Jaren. Clyde stepped in between Jaren and the approaching Gex with his sword ready. The Gex went for an overhead swing which Clyde successfully blocked with his sword. The swing was powerful and heavy, so Clyde angled his sword so that the Gex slid off toward the ground, knocking it off balance for a moment.

Clyde used that moment to pull his kukri out and jammed it right under the Gex's arm as deep as he could go. Clyde's aim was good as the Gex fell to the ground dead. Clyde looked back to the others, and they had finished them off with ease it seemed.

"Well, that definitely went better than the last time I fought them," said Clyde as he sat down feeling exhausted.

"Well, to be fair, it would take quite a bit more to kill my boys here," said Jaren as he sat beside Clyde.

"Listen my boy, I heard the story of your last encounter. First of all, they had no business going through this area as they were given explicit instructions to avoid it. Secondly, you were unprepared to protect such a large group of people that you just happened to come across while you were out here. So don't weigh your mind down with the nonsense that it was your fault. They died because they were unprepared. The few that survived is because you decided to help with everything you could," lectured Jaren.

Clyde could only nod in response, and it seemed to be a satisfactory answer for Jaren as he stood to his feet.

"Just think, you've successfully protected me just a few minutes ago and I didn't have to lift a finger. Don't be so hard on yourself," said Jaren as he offered a hand to Clyde.

"Right... we'll take a break here and grab the valuables from these carcasses before traveling a few more miles," said Clyde as Jaren helped him to his feet.

Clyde spent the next few hours carving up the dead Gex and making a makeshift sled out of the Gex parts and some rope he had brought. Clyde had started to pull it along as they started traveling again when Tug stopped him.

"I'll drag this. You save your energy to make us another yummy dinner," he said as he grabbed the rope to the sled.

"Alright. I'll make something extra special when we set up camp then," Clyde said, making Drue and Tug visibly excited.

Since it was the last night they were going to camp, Clyde used what provisions he had left as well as some Gex meat to make a hearty stew for everyone. Clyde had learned from Skye how to cook the tough but only slimy Gex meat and make it taste quite delicious as well. It seemed that Clyde made it just as intended because even Jarren was asking for a second bowl.

After one more cold night in No Man's Land, they had finally made it to the town and to Clyde's relief, it was in one piece.

"Well, I do believe that is a job well done. We have arrived safely and I'm still quite ahead of schedule," Jaren said as he shook Clyde's hand.

"Now I require a drink in a warm place before we settle things. Please lead the way, Clyde my boy," he said, pushing Clyde along.

Clyde took them to Darren's shop where he felt most comfortable talking about any sort of business.

"Welco... well, look who's finally dragged themselves back," Darren said as he greeted Clyde with a hearty pat on the shoulders.

"Would you happen to have a room in the back open so I could talk some business with my client," Clyde asked Darren before he got carried away with questions.

"Oh, I see. Yea, the usual room is still clean. Do you need any drinks," asked Darren.

"Yes, bring some of your special stuff you hide in the back," said Clyde as he directed Jaren to the small cozy room in the back of the store.

Clyde, Jarren, Tug, and Drue sat in the small room and, soon after, Darren came in with a bottle of expensive wine and some dried meat and cheese.

"Alrighty. So, the agreed price was one hundred and twenty gold neros and you have already received half, yes," asked Jaren as he took an appreciated sip of wine.

"Yes, you owe me sixty gold," Clyde said as he caught a glimpse of Darren looking at him in shock.

"Well, I have a proposal for you, Clyde my boy," Jaren said after putting his cup down.

"Proposal," questioned Clyde.

"Yes... I need to deliver a message to my caravan that should arrive in this town in about two months along with, I think, three other slave caravans heading south," said Jaren.

"And you want me to deliver this message," asked Clyde, after he took a sip of the wine himself.

"Yes. I want you to let the caravan head, Aribold, know that I went on ahead of him and give him this letter as well," said Jaren, producing a wax sealed letter and placing it on the table.

"If you wish to earn another fifteen gold as well as two written favors from me personally, all you gotta do is deliver that message and this letter to Aribold," Jaren said confidently.

"What do you mean by favors," asked Clyde.

"Ahh, I'll give you two sealed letters that you can either give me or any of my associates in any of the locations I own and whatever you need at the time, if it's within my power to help you with, I'll help you free of charge," said Jaren right before draining the contents of his cup.

Clyde wasn't really sure how handy the favors would be, but the fifteen gold was more than enough for him to deliver a message, so he reached his hand out toward Jaren.

"Very well. I'll deliver your message," Clyde said as Jarren took Clyde's hand with both of his.

"Wonderful. I knew I could count on you, my boy. Say, if you wish to have a solid job, don't hesitate to follow the caravan. I'll hire you on the spot," said Jaren happily.

Clyde felt a bit undeserving at the praise but couldn't help himself from smiling at the thought.

"How long do you plan to stay in this town," Clyde asked as they were leaving the room.

"Only till morning. I'm afraid we've still got quite a way to travel, and I'd like to get there as soon as possible so I don't miss anything," Jarren said.

"What exactly were you going south for again," Clyde asked out of curiosity.

"Oh, there's apparently a meeting between all the large slavers on the Dwarven border. I'm not sure what it's about but there's supposed to be a large auction as well so I can't pass up getting some good deals whilst I'm there," said Jaren as he turned toward Darren.

"Alrighty shopkeeper, I require a week's worth of traveling supplies and rations by tomorrow morning. Is that possible," Jaren asked suddenly.

"Oh... yes, I'm sure I could find what you need by then," Darren said as he was already getting some of the things together.

"Now then, we need a place to sleep for the night," Jaren said, turning towards Clyde.

"Ahh, right, there's a tavern at the end of town that has some rooms. I'll show you the way," Clyde said before they began toward the tavern.

It was almost dusk when they left Darren's store and headed toward the tavern. About halfway there, Jaren began to speak again.

"Really Clyde, I want you to know how much I appreciate how much you've done for me. I'm truly surprised you even agreed to escort me, let alone help me so much," Jaren said, seeming almost apologetic.

"I should be the one thanking you. It's hard to tell how long I would have let that bother me... even though it still does. You've helped me realize that I need to keep moving on and just do better next time," Clyde said as he continued down the street as the lamplighter had begun lighting the streetlamps.

"Well, here you all ar... ahh!!" Clyde couldn't finish his sentence as Tug had picked him up, embracing Clyde in a tight strangling hug.

"I don't wanna say bye to our cook, Boss. I promise I'll take care of him," pleaded Tug as Clyde helplessly struggled to breathe.

"Now Tug, put him down. I'm sure we'll be meeting him again sometime," Jaren said, looking unworried.

Tug listened almost immediately as he sat Clyde back down allowing him to catch his breath.

"Clyde, my boy, it's been a pleasure," Jaren said, holding his hand out toward Clyde.

"Likewise. I look forward to the next we meet," said Clyde as he shook Jaren's hand

Clyde left them at the tavern and headed home to see Skye and Skaald. He was relieved that he had almost a month to relax and recover from his last adventure. Thinkin about it though, he was almost eager to see what his next one would be.

Epilogue: The Caravan and the Slave

Over the month break, Clyde had simply tended to his gear and equipment then continued to help Skaald and Skye with chores. Skye made sure Clyde kept up with his reading as he borrowed books from Oliver every chance he could to learn more about magic and the different aspects of this new world. He found the history of the elves to be fairly interesting. Seeing as though Oliver didn't have many books about them, Clyde only knew the general history of what happened to them. Apparently, they came from a large Elven nation far across the southern sea and settled next to the Dwarven nation. Then when the Humans began the war with the Lizardians, they attempted to conquer the Elves' land as well but with no success as they failed multiple times. Oddly enough, Clyde couldn't find any details as to why or how they failed so it left him to wonder. Along with his reading and chores, he began writing and receiving letters from Pix as well. At first the letters were hard to read and had plenty of mistakes; even so, Clyde always looked forward to seeing what would be in her next letter. Clyde sent a book to Pix along with almost every letter he sent her, hopefully to keep her mind sharp and to never run out of new things to talk to Clyde about. From her letters, it seemed as though the old shopkeeper talked her into wearing a dress instead of her traveling clothes fairly early on and although she said that the old man was harsh and stubborn with his lessons with every letter Clyde got, he could definitely tell she was improving fast. No sooner than he received the fifth letter by messenger bird from Pix, a month had come and went almost before Clyde could realize. He was helping Skye deliver her medicine through the town when they saw the large caravan arrive. There must have been twenty wagons with at least four horsemen per wagon and five people walking with each wagon. It was by far the largest caravan Clyde had ever seen before. On closer inspection, they all seemed to be carrying the same cargo... slaves. There was one wagon in particular that stood out to Clyde though and it was simply a large metal cage with a single person in it. Upon closer inspection, it seemed to be a young girl in it which stood out like a sore thumb to Clyde.

"I suppose I've got to go deliver this message. I'll see you at the house later this evening," Clyde said to Skye before heading over to the caravan.

Clyde approached the caravan and almost immediately began to get suspicious looks from almost everyone in the caravan. He tried to shrug them off as he looked for someone approachable to speak to. He came across a man upon a horse that was giving some directions to some men. After he finished, Clyde approached him. "Excuse me, Sir, could you help me with something," Clyde asked as the man twirled his horse to face Clyde.

"Aye, what is it, boy," asked the man quickly.

Clyde didn't really appreciate being called a boy, but he figured it could be worse as he continued.

"I'm looking for a man by the name of Aribold. I have a message for him," said Clyde loudly so the man could hear him over the rising noise of the caravan setting up for the night.

"Ahh, that'll be me then. Come. We'll talk over yonder," he said as he turned his horse and began trotting off.

Clyde followed him to a large wagon that seemed almost like a circus wagon. On the inside though, it simply seemed to be living quarters. Everything inside seemed to be secured by either ropes or nailed down so it wouldn't slide around whilst it moved. Everything seemed to be quite organized as well, almost meticulously. As Clyde stepped in, Aribold motioned for Clyde to sit across from him. Once they had both sat down, Clyde produced the sealed letter from Jaren.

"Right, then let's just see what this message is," he said as he broke the seal and began to read.

The longer he read, the more his expression changed. It went from an easygoing expression to more of an upset or angry expression the longer he read the letter.

"Is everything alright," asked Clyde, who immediately wanted to leave as soon as he opened his mouth.

"I wish the boss would understand that him running off leaving me in charge is more trouble than it's possibly worth in the first place but now he's giving me errands to do on top of all the work he's already left me," he said, right before letting out a long, irritated sigh.

"Well, from my limited time with him, I can understand how he could be frustrating to work for… if there isn't anything else, I believe I'll take my…"

"Well, actually, he asked me to offer you a job to work under me with the caravan… And he explicitly said to try and be persistent," Aribold said cutting Clyde off.

"I'm afraid I'll have to decline… Although I know the pay is well and all, I don't really see myself working for a slaver in good conscience," said Clyde, hoping the man wasn't going to be as persistent as Jaren.

"Well, I tried... If you change your mind of course, I'm positive the boss will hire you. He doesn't forget people he likes, trust me," he said as he folded the letter neatly and placed it in a drawer that must have been full of them.

"Well, if you're sure you don't want a job, I suppose I've got no reason to hold ya here. It's been a pleasure," he said as he pulled out some other papers and began going through them.

Clyde took his opportunity to leave. "Likewise, and good luck in your travels," Clyde said as he opened the door Aribold looked up to him and smiled as Clyde shut the door behind him.

The day was coming to a close as dusk was fast approaching. Clyde could hear some kind of commotion coming from within the convoy. Thinking about it, he figured it would be best to just ignore it and head home. He held his cloak tightly as the cold night's winter air was unforgiving as it blew through the backstreets which Clyde was traversing on his way home. Clyde couldn't help but think out loud to himself as he walked.

"I wonder if another opportunity for an adventure will come? It's hard to pass up a job that offers both good pay and interesting adventures like that. I suppose I had better not let the next opportunity slip by me or else I'll fall into my old workaholic habits again," Clyde said as he gazed upwards at the stars shining in between the buildings.

No sooner had he taken a few more careless steps than he felt something run into him with a thud. Luckily, it was still light enough outside for Clyde to clearly see the person in question. Currently laying in the mud and snow was a girl. She was small in size, but Clyde could tell that she was no child from the look in her eyes. She was wearing tattered rags as clothes and no shoes in the middle of winter. On her ankles and wrists were cuffs attached to chains just long enough for her to maybe half run, which seemed to be what she was doing from her heavy breathing and all. Clyde then quit examining her as he caught her half angry, half scared gaze. Her eyes were a burning bright yellow and her ears were pointed and long. She was obviously an Elf. Clyde was about to say something when she spoke first.

"Neshanas staring at Salen. Talas va / var (pl) siffi ent. Help me," she said in Elvish as she began to stand.

Clyde understood the insult completely; however, she was somewhat justified as Clyde did stare at her for a while. He thought to himself that he needed to quit wishing things upon himself. He briefly considered what he was about to get into. *This girl was obviously a runaway slave and would be a ton of trouble for him as well. But Clyde couldn't just not help her on other hand,* Clyde's thoughts were interrupted by the sound of men shouting.

"She must have gone this way!! Don't stop until you've found her!!" The shouting was followed by footsteps closing in fast.

"Well, I suppose I was asking for an adventure."

A Note to the Reader

Hello readers, this is the author here. I hope you enjoyed Clyde's story so far. This is my first book of hopefully many. I've always wanted to put my own story out there. I enjoy thinking up all kinds of adventures to the point that I began running campaigns of Dungeons and Dragons for my friends. I would like to thank all of my friends for pushing me to complete this book and move forward with getting it published. I would also like to thank all of you readers and, hopefully, new fans of my world I've begun forging. I hope by the time the next volume is ready, you all will be excited to see what happens next in Clyde's story.